Monster Doughnuts

CYCLOPS ON A MISSION

GIANNA POLLERO

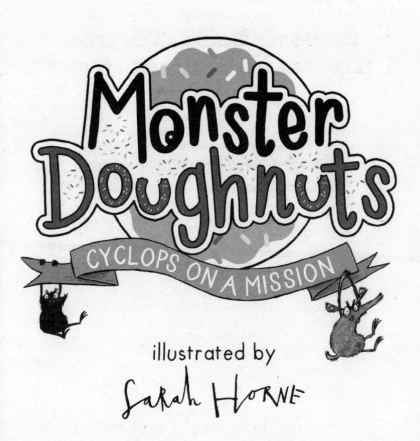

Monster Doughnuts

CYCLOPS ON A MISSION

illustrated by

Sarah Horne

Piccadilly
PRESS

First published in Great Britain in 2022 by
PICCADILLY PRESS
4th Floor, Victoria House, Bloomsbury Square, London WC1B 4DA
Owned by Bonnier Books
Sveavägen 56, Stockholm, Sweden
www.piccadillypress.co.uk

A CIP catalogue record for this book is available from the British Library.

ISBN: 978-1-80078-084-2
Also available in ebook and audio

3

Designed by Suzanne Cooper
Printed and bound in Great Britain by Clays Ltd, Elcograf S.p.A.

Piccadilly Press is an imprint of Bonnier Books UK
www.bonnierbooks.co.uk

For my mum, who I couldn't do without,
and for my dad, who I miss every day

CHAPTER ONE

Grace vs the Bath Dweller

Grace yanked the tentacle out of her nose and wiped the trail of snot-like slime off her face, as she held the squirming monster at arm's length over the bath. The master bathroom in the House by the River was usually gleaming white and peaceful. Today, not so much.

'Mr Harris!' she yelled. 'For goodness' sake! HELP!'

The cyclops lowered the TV magazine he was holding and peered over the top. 'What's the matter?' he replied impatiently. 'I'm trying to read.'

Grace slapped another tentacle away from her ear with her free hand and turned her head just in time to avoid a squirt of foul-smelling liquid. 'What do you think is the matter? Look! You're meant to be learning how to do this! We're on a training exercise!' she cried. 'This Bath Dweller is crazy. It has more tentacles than I've ever seen and I'm struggling to get it under control! You're just sitting there reading, when you should be helping!'

Mr Harris raised the magazine back in front of his face and muttered from behind it, 'I am learning. I know that Bath Dwellers are not dangerous. The worst they can do is stick their tentacles to you and squirt you with grotty water. So stop making a fuss.'

Grace shook her head wildly in an attempt to get at least four tentacles out of her long, dark hair. 'You say they're not dangerous, but what if it puts its tentacles over my nose and mouth? What would happen then?'

Mr Harris lowered the magazine again. 'Oh, well then you would die.'

'Then HELP ME! I've got no hands left to get the lemon meringue pie!' shouted Grace, clamping her mouth shut as another tentacle prodded her lip.

The cyclops snapped the magazine shut. 'That's bad planning. You should never put yourself in that position. And you've ruined my 'me' time. You're so dramatic, Doughnut Lady! *Oh, it could kill me. Oh, it has so many tentacles. Oh, where's my exploding cake? Oh, help me, amazing Mr Harris, help me . . .*' He tutted and shook his enormous head.

If one of Grace's hands had been free, she would have slapped him. Despite his vastness, and his tendency to eat people and other monsters with very little warning, she wasn't remotely scared of him. She was a twelfth-generation monster-hunter, after all. And since they had been thrust together in an unlikely friendship, after they had saved the Prime Minister's life just the week before, she was oddly fond of the obnoxious creature.

Grace closed her eyes as the Bath Dweller's tentacles suckered almost every part of her face to try to make her release her grip. She didn't see Mr Harris heave his feet off the wooden stool and shuffle over. Suddenly, Grace felt all the pressure from the suckers disappear. Some even made popping sounds as they were lifted from her skin. She opened her eyes, to see Mr Harris looming in front of her.

'Gone. I don't know what all the fuss was about,' said Mr Harris, licking the end of his massive finger.

'Did you *eat* it?' Grace asked.

Mr Harris belched. 'Yuck. Tasted like tuna that's gone off. I wouldn't recommend that you sample one.'

'Why would you eat it? They stink!' Grace said in disbelief.

'What else did you want me to do with it?' Mr Harris snapped. 'Put a bonnet on it and pop it on my shoulder? You were all screechy and it was the quickest way to get rid of it. And not a word of thanks from you. Anyway, I was hungry.'

'You're always hungry,' said Grace, rolling her eyes. 'And thank you.'

Mr Harris frowned, then sniggered.

'What?' asked Grace. 'What's funny?'

'Your face is funny.' He giggled. 'You have spots all over it where it stuck its suckers to you. You look DISGUSTING. But funny.'

'Great,' said Grace flatly. 'Glad I amuse you. You do realise you can't do this when you officially start working for the Secret Service next week?'

'Do what?' the cyclops asked irritably.

'Have 'me' time while you're out on a monster-hunting mission. You'll either have to get the job done on your own or you'll have to work as part of a team. Either way, you'll have to put in a lot of effort all the time,' said Grace.

'I am too important to work as part of a team,' the cyclops said smugly. 'I saved the Prime Minister's life *and* destroyed my evil grandfather before he ate her. All in the space of a few minutes. I am a hero, Doughnut Lady. I will probably just have to sit in a great big office and sign things.'

'*We* saved the Prime Minister's life and destroyed your grandfather, Neville. And, seriously, you start on Monday – have you not read your job description yet? You're a part-time field officer working for the Secret Service. That means you'll have to go out and do actual missions – although why you're only part-time, I have no idea. You were offered the job because of your monster knowledge – you know, what with you being one yourself. You'll never just be in an office!' said Grace.

'You don't know anything,' said Mr Harris.

'I know that you'll be on the front line,' Grace said. 'It'll be hard work and it'll be dangerous. You really need to read the information, Mr Harris.'

'You can help me,' he replied flatly.

'Not really,' said Grace. 'I'm only working with you over the summer holidays to show you what to do. Then I'll be back at school and you'll have to carry on without me.'

'Fine. You're annoying. I'll be glad of the break,' the cyclops mumbled.

'Well, you've got five more weeks of me yet!' said Grace cheerfully. 'Right, let's go downstairs and find Frank. He'll be pleased the Bath Dweller has gone.'

CHAPTER TWO

Mr Harris
and the Monster Scanner

Mr Harris's large yellow eye nearly popped out
of his big green head when the door to the
office opened. They were in the cellar of Max
and Frank's house. The vast space was home to
two sleek white desks, two huge black leather
swivel chairs and so many screens that it was like
being in a television shop. Whiteboards were
positioned around the room, many covered in
pictures of monsters and information, some with
string joining them together.

'I assume this is my office?' said Mr Harris
smugly.

'Ha! In your dreams,' said Grace. 'Hey, Frank! The Bath Dweller has gone.'

One of the big black chairs swivelled round to reveal a small boy with curly blond hair, holding an ornate golden fork in one hand.

Mr Harris baulked. 'You have to be kidding. Tell me this is not Shrimp Boy's office.'

Frank waved his fork. 'Hi, Grace!' he said, then slightly more nervously, he added, 'And h-hello, Mr Harris.'

'Shrimp Boy.' Mr Harris nodded curtly.

'How did the training exercise go?' Frank asked.

'I smashed it,' said Mr Harris.

Grace shook her head. 'No, you ate it.'

'You ate the B-B-Bath Dweller?' Frank asked, gesturing towards Mr Harris with his fork.

'Yes,' said Mr Harris. 'I saved Doughnut Lady's life. Again. The Bath Dweller was about to put its tentacles up her big nostrils and into her bossy mouth so I had to act fast.'

Grace snorted. 'You fibber! You were reading a magazine! And you ate the monster because you were hungry and too lazy to dispose of it properly.'

Mr Harris folded his arms across his chest and pulled himself up to his full height.

'Please don't argue!' Frank interjected. 'It makes me n-nervous. If the Bath Dweller has gone, it's fine, whatever happened. Mr Harris, I'm going to show you how to file it as dead on the Monster Scanner.'

At the mention of the Monster Scanner, Mr Harris's eye widened, full of interest. He shuffled over towards Frank, wheeling the other black chair with him. He pushed it right up to Frank's so the arm rests were touching, and plopped his enormous body into the seat.

Grace could tell Frank was nervous. His fork, which he carried at all times for protection, and which was the only thing he'd kept from his time living with goblins in Monster World, was trembling. At ten, Grace was only two years older than him, but she was so proud of how much braver he had become since she had met him for the first time, just a few weeks before.

Frank clicked in the search field, typed 'Bath Dweller' and said, 'When you don't know a monster's full name, you can put in the details you do know – here. Or you can put a picture into this slot, or some of its DNA – like a tuft of fur or a claw – in here.' He gestured to a hi-tech Perspex dish.

'Right you are,' said Mr Harris. With no warning, he spat a green-tinged glob of saliva into the dish. Grace put her hand over her nose and mouth, partly in shock, and partly because of the foul smell. Frank's eyes welled up, as if he might cry. Or vomit.

'You're welcome,' said Mr Harris. 'Plenty DNA in there.'

The dish moved, on a dainty mechanical arm, into a slot in the side of the machine. It hummed and whirred, and the screen went blank briefly, before a full monster profile burst into life.

Name: Squidmund Strongsuckers

Type: Bath Dweller

Age: 17 years

Height: 62 cm

Weight: 16 lb

Strengths: 5 detected: speed, strength, number of tentacles, freestyle swimming strokes, card games.

Weaknesses: 3 detected: unintelligent, easily confused, can't breathe for long out of water.

Likes: Water, bubble bath, magic, street dance, synchronised swimming, citrus fruit.

Dislikes: Dry land, fish and chip shops, bath crayons, Monopoly.

Best form of destruction: Meringue containing excess baking powder.

Notes: Bath Dwellers can make themselves very small to hide, and expand when fully immersed in bath water. Check plugholes thoroughly.

SCORING:

Friendship: 12

Size: 31

Courage: 41

Kindness: 8

Intelligence: 7

Loyalty: 2

Violence: 57

Danger: 39

Type: Common, especially in densely populated areas.

OPTIONS:

• Add notes

• Add sighting

• Move to 'Dead' folder

Additional notes: Secondary DNA identified, belonging to:

cyclops, Mr Harris. *Click here for more details*.

CHAPTER THREE

Cyclopes Don't Like Paperwork

'That's me!' cried Mr Harris, leaning forward. 'I am in this important machine! Click for more information, Shrimp Boy! Come on!'

'Not now, Mr Harris,' said Grace. 'You need to learn how to file a dead monster. I can show you your profile another time.'

Mr Harris breathed loudly through his nostrils in annoyance and folded his arms again.

'So, you click here and enter the details, and the time and date of the monster's destruction,' Frank said, hovering the mouse over the 'Move to "Dead" folder' option.

'Well, yes, that's very hard, isn't it? When a monster is dead, you file it in the "Dead" folder,' said Mr Harris. 'I can completely see why Doughnut Lady wanted me to concentrate on such a difficult piece of information, instead of viewing my own very important profile.'

Grace ignored him and turned instead to Frank. 'Do you have the forms Mr Harris needs to fill in before he starts next week? He could do them while he's here, so we can help.'

'I won't need help,' spat Mr Harris. 'Hand them over.'

Frank hooked the paper-clipped documents onto the end of his fork from a tray at the far end of the desk and held them out to the cyclops. Within seconds Mr Harris was moaning.

'Why do they need all this information? It's ridiculous. I am too important, and valuable, to be writing things on forms. Give me a proper job . . .'

'Actually, you'll be getting your first official assignments later on,' said Max, appearing in the doorway, waving at Grace with his right hand. His left hand – and arm – were missing, injured irreparably in a monster hunt years before.

'Max!' cried Grace, running over to give Frank's dad – who was her own dad's cousin – a big hug.

'Hey, Grace!' said Max. 'How did the training go?'

'Spectacularly well,' called Mr Harris from Max's desk, where he was sitting.

'Other than you eating the t-target,' Frank ventured bravely. The cyclops huffed loudly and scribbled aggressively on the papers in front of him.

Grace high-fived Frank then turned to Max. 'So, what are you working on now?'

Before Max could answer, a ballpoint pen whistled past his face and hit the floor by Grace's feet. She looked up to see Mr Harris staring at her. He appeared to be cross.

'Are you having trouble with your form? Do you want me to help?' She walked over to him and peered over his shoulder. 'Good grief, your writing is awful.'

Mr Harris stared at her. 'That's very rude. I'm sure your writing is uglier. I can hardly help the fact that my strong hands find it challenging to

hold these cheap, horrible plastic pens.' He held up another black biro between his finger and thumb as if it was a dead rat. 'Did trolls source them? They are cheap creatures.'

'Give it to me. I'll do it,' said Grace, pulling up a chair and sweeping the form along the desk towards her.

Mr Harris's writing was as large and unkempt as he was. The letters he had scrawled spanned a good couple of lines: some were quite neat, some looked like hieroglyphics.

'Okay,' said Grace, 'so you've filled in your name and your date of birth. Hang on a minute – I thought you had no middle names?'

The cyclops grinned. 'I've added my own, seeing as no one could be bothered to give me proper ones.'

'And what a lovely choice!' said Grace, sniggering. 'Let's see, Steven Florian Severin

Alberto Prometheus Colin Harris. The fourth. Apparently.'

Mr Harris nodded smugly. 'That's me.'

Max and Frank stifled giggles from the other desk then, seeing the look on the cyclops's face, quickly turned away and busied themselves with some photos of a team of Parent Punishers, reported as being 'loose and wild' in Kensington.

'Your choice, I suppose,' said Grace. 'Now let's see, date of birth . . . you've put *June, sixteen sixty-something, probably.* You can't put that as a date of birth!'

'Why?' demanded Mr Harris. 'I *was* born in sixteen sixty-something.'

'Well, let's try and make it more specific. Which date in June?' said Grace patiently.

'The forty-seventh,' Mr Harris replied.

Grace sighed. 'June has thirty days, Mr Harris. I'll put the thirtieth.'

'I still prefer the forty-seventh,' said the cyclops, folding his arms.

Grace took a deep breath. 'Moving on . . . right, family details. Full names of mother, father, siblings and maternal and paternal grandparents.'

'This is so boring.' The cyclops groaned. 'Father, Egbert Marcus Gerald Otis Endeavour Bryan – dead. Siblings, none. Grandparents, probably all dead. Neville Adolphus Quentin Timothy Artemis Clarence Harris, as you know, is definitely dead, because I – I mean we – exploded the scaly old reptile.' He smiled triumphantly.

Grace nodded, thinking back to the dramatic scene in the Prime Minister's office just a couple of weeks before. 'So, that leaves your mum, assuming she's alive? What's her name?'

'She is alive,' snapped Mr Harris. 'Gertrudetta Millicent Patricia Juanita Mavis Carole Harris. She's actually quite a delightful cyclops. It's just a shame she liked Neville so much.'

'Well, he was her dad, I suppose,' mumbled Grace, as she wrote the names down as quickly as she could. 'It says here you need to provide the last-known home address and occupation for all living relatives.'

The cyclops frowned. 'Last I knew, she was a teacher.'

'A teacher?' asked Grace, glancing up.

'Yes. A teacher. The Harris family of cyclopes is not stupid, Doughnut Lady,' he shot back.

'That's not what I meant,' Grace replied, intrigued. 'I'm just surprised she's a teacher. Does she teach in Monster World?'

The cyclops sighed loudly. 'Always so many questions. You're so very, very nosy. When I last saw her, she was teaching here in Human World.'

'Here?' Grace yelped.

'Yes,' said Mr Harris. 'Most monsters are thick and not very many go to school, so there's not much point in teaching there. And don't worry – she's a vegetarian.'

Grace raised her eyebrows. 'Is she not, well, noticeable? Since she's a cyclops?'

Mr Harris shook his head in disgust. 'You know from my own excellent disguises that she would have no problem appearing to be human.

'Wow,' said Grace, her mind racing at the thought of a cyclops disguised as a teacher. Vegetarian or not, she was related to Mr Harris. 'Okay, let's carry on with this form. Where does she live?'

'I don't know, I haven't spoken to her for some time. We don't speak any more. Probably by the sea. She likes the sea,' the cyclops said sniffily. Then he mumbled, 'Although I've checked everywhere and I can't find her.'

'*By the sea* is probably not enough for the form so I'll just put *address unknown*,' Grace said. 'And, actually, thinking about it, we didn't put in your address, did we?'

'I'm not divulging my personal place of dwelling,' said Mr Harris arrogantly. 'Just put down your address.'

'Fine,' said Grace, scribbling down the address of her family bakery, Cake Hunters. 'But where *do* you live? I've never thought to ask.'

The cyclops paused. 'I live in hotels,' he said. 'Nice ones, obviously, with room service and big televisions so I can watch *Britain's Got Talent.*'

'What do you mean, you live in hotels?' asked Grace. 'Where are you finding the money to live in London hotels? They cost a fortune for just one night!'

'I don't need any money,' Mr Harris said self-importantly. 'They never make me pay.'

'Oh my goblins,' whispered Frank. 'Do you eat the staff?'

'Of course I don't,' hissed Mr Harris. 'I'm not a monster, Shrimp Boy.' He cast his eye to the floor and mumbled, 'I just . . . quickly . . . you know, hypnotise them . . . it's fine . . . no harm done . . .'

'Steven Florian Severin Alberto Prometheus Colin Harris the fourth!' said Grace. 'You cannot hypnotise people to get things for free! It's wrong. And rude. And you absolutely, definitely can't do it now you work for the Prime Minister! Enough is enough.' She shook her head. 'I think I'm probably going to regret saying this but, Mr Harris, as of today, you're coming to live with me. At Cake Hunters.'

CHAPTER FOUR

Monster Lodge

Grace waited until she knew the bakery would be closed before she brought Mr Harris to his new home. She had to call him twice to get him to stop staring at the delicious offerings in Cake Hunters' window and actually come inside.

'I'm home! And we have a guest!' she shouted as she closed the door and locked it. Mr Harris looked round the homely bakery in awe. His gaze moved slowly across the cake stands and gingham display trays before lingering on the mound of doughnuts behind the counter. His eye grew wide at the sight of a tower of profiteroles marked *Display only, specialist patisserie – please ask for more details.*

'Grace, you're back! Look what Danni and I made! A rainbow cake!' said Grace's mum, Louisa, rushing into the bakery from upstairs, gesturing towards a magnificent, vibrant and colourful cake on the counter. She stopped at the unexpected sight of the cyclops, who had once eaten both her and Grace's dad. 'Oh, Mr Harris! Hello.'

Mr Harris tipped his hat as a greeting, too distracted by the mention of a rainbow cake to speak. Grace's sister, Danni, and her dad, Eamon, appeared a few seconds later and fell silent when they saw the cyclops, now with his back to them, perusing the croissants.

'Why is he here?' mouthed Danni to Grace, pointing.

Mr Harris curled his huge arm over the top of

the counter and helped himself to three almond croissants at lightning speed before turning round to face the Hunter family.

'Doughnut Lady said I need to live here,' he said, dropping the first croissant into his enormous gullet.

No sound came from the open mouths of Grace's parents and sister.

Mr Harris continued, 'So, please show me to my room. I assume it has a very small fridge with nuts in it?'

'Live here?' Louisa said. Her voice came out as a squeak.

'I know!' Grace said. 'But I'll take responsibility for him. And he promised on the way here to be on his best behaviour. There's no chance he'll eat any of us, with all these cakes around!'

Eamon nodded, the same way someone would nod if they were told they had to have their sore tooth extracted with no anaesthetic. Danni moved closer to her mum.

Mr Harris grinned and scoffed another croissant.

'And I think it makes sense to keep an eye on him while he's working with us,' Grace added encouragingly. When Mr Harris turned to help himself to another croissant, she looked at her family and mouthed, 'I'm so sorry!'

'Right, yes, I can see how that makes some sort of sense,' said Louisa, snapping herself out of her shock. 'He can stay in the other attic room. That has an old bed in it. I'll go and make it up, and see if I can find some nuts . . .' She bustled off upstairs.

The movement seemed to jolt Danni and Eamon into life. Danni disappeared behind the bakery counter to replenish the croissants for the following day, and Eamon gestured for Grace and Mr Harris to come and sit at one of the tables at the back of the room.

'So, Mr Harris, I have your assignments here,' said Eamon, holding up a large brown envelope marked *CONFIDENTIAL*. 'Would you like to see?'

The cyclops leaned forward eagerly and snatched the envelope.

Eamon raised his eyebrows and smiled at Grace. 'There's an urgent case we need to get to work on right away, and another we can take a little more time with because the police are already investigating. Grace, I'm going to need your help on both of these too. I've already asked Max and Frank to lend a hand.'

Grace nodded, watching Mr Harris rip open the envelope and thrust his hand inside. His eye was sparkly and wide with excitement.

'Case one three seven five B,' he read slowly. 'Urgent. A monster, believed to be a Bottom Biter, appears to be making its way directly from Monster World into London. He steals food and other products. He has also bitten a significant number of people on the bottom (latest figure, twenty-seven), causing an itchy, angry purple rash. News of this monster CANNOT under ANY circumstances reach the British media.

So far, no journalists are known to have been bitten. The mission is to find the monster's point of entry into London, then locate the monster and destroy it at the earliest opportunity.'

Mr Harris sniggered. 'A Bottom Biter.'

Grace rolled her eyes. 'They might sound funny, but they're awful creatures. A cross between a Shadow Stalker and a vampire bat. What's the other case?'

Mr Harris pulled out another piece of paper. 'Case one one nine two A. Intelligence-gathering operation with Scotland Yard, investigating . . . oh. Well, I don't think this one is particularly important.' He stuffed the paper back into the envelope and was about to sit on it when Grace snatched it out of his huge hand.

She unfolded it and continued to read. 'Investigating the disappearance of the head judge in popular prime-time TV series, *Britain's Got Talent*. He was last seen on his way to dinner, following auditions at the London Palladium.'

CHAPTER FIVE

Mr Harris Settles In

'I remember reading about this!' said Grace. 'He literally vanished into thin air. No one has seen him or heard from him in weeks.'

'He's probably on holiday,' said Mr Harris dismissively. 'I don't know what all the fuss is about.'

'He would have told someone if he was going away,' said Grace. 'There's definitely something suspicious going on.'

'I think you've read too many detective stories, Doughnut Lady,' said Mr Harris, whipping the case file out of her hand and replacing it with

the one about the Bottom Biter. 'This is the important one. All those poor bottoms.' He giggled.

Before Grace could remind him they needed to investigate both cases, her mum appeared from upstairs. 'Mr Harris, your room is ready,' she said. 'Do you want to take your things up before dinner?' She looked at his battered leather suitcase and the blue bag for life at his feet.

'Dinner?' he said, lowering the magazine, immediately interested.

Louisa nodded. 'Yes, you're welcome to join us. We eat here in the bakery. It's lasagne tonight, with a nice green salad and as much fresh bread as you like.'

Mr Harris licked his lips. 'Lasagne? Isn't that like a layered cake?'

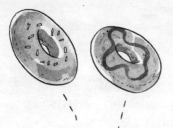

'Yes, if you layer your cakes with pasta!' Grace laughed, putting the papers down and standing up. 'Come on then, let's get your stuff up to your room.'

'But I don't want to be late for dinner. That would be rude,' said Mr Harris.

'You won't be,' replied Grace. 'We'll only be upstairs for five minutes. There's not much to show you – it's pretty snug.'

'Fine,' said Mr Harris huffily. 'But I don't want to miss dinner. You don't want me to get hungry.'

Grace raised her eyebrows. 'I hope that wasn't a threat, Mr Harris. If you eat any of us *again*, you'll definitely lose your job at the Secret Service.'

The cyclops shook his head. 'I didn't mean I'd eat *you*. You said yourself, why would I eat you when all these cakes are here? They will taste so much better!'

'I'd rather you said you wouldn't eat us at all, but fine,' mumbled Grace.

'Let's see my room, then,' said Mr Harris, stomping off to the door that led upstairs.

'Yes, let's . . . I'll take these, shall I?' replied Grace, picking up the bags he had left on the floor. At the top of the stairs, she wiped sweat from her forehead. 'What have you got in these?' she asked. 'They weigh a ton!'

'My personal belongings,' said Mr Harris. 'Which door?'

'The one to the left,' Grace said, out of breath. 'The other one is our office.'

Mr Harris peered in. 'Is that one of those scanners?'

'Yes, it's a Monster Scanner. It's not quite as advanced as Max and Frank's but it does pretty much the same thing,' said Grace. Seeing how interested Mr Harris looked, she pulled the door closed, crossed the cramped landing and opened the door opposite.

'Here's your room,' she said.

The space was small, with sloping ceilings and a comfy window seat. The bed had an old iron frame and a patchwork quilt. Louisa had thoughtfully left a packet of honey roast cashew nuts on the plump white pillow and a small can of Lynx deodorant on the bedside table – cyclopes

had a tendency to smell less than pleasant. There was a desk pushed into the far corner of the room, with a lamp on it, and a chest of drawers pushed up against the desk. It would have been cosy for someone half the size of the cyclops.

Mr Harris was quiet for what seemed like a long time. 'I'll take it,' he said. 'It reminds me of my first cave.'

Grace wasn't sure if that was a good thing or not. She put his bags by the foot of the bed. 'I'll leave you to unpack,' she said.

'I never unpack,' said Mr Harris, squeezing the brown leather suitcase into a drawer, then the bag for life into the one underneath. 'There, all done. Dinner time!'

CHAPTER SIX

How Many Fairies in a Fairy Cake?

Grace woke reluctantly and squinted at the clock on her bedside table. 9.12 a.m.

'Oh no,' she mumbled, 'we're meant to leave for Max and Frank's at half past.' She scrambled out of bed and pulled on a pair of jeans and a stripy T-shirt. She had stayed up late with her dad, researching Bottom Biters, checking through old journals and scraps of information.

Her notes clutched in her hand, she raced up the stairs to the attic to tell Mr Harris what she had discovered. She knocked on the door. There was no response, so she knocked louder. And then louder still. But all was silent. Grace turned the doorknob and opened the door just enough to see inside. The bed was made neatly and there was no sign whatsoever of a 280-lb cyclops.

'Oh no.' Grace groaned. 'Where is he?' She raced downstairs and flung open the door to the bakery, hoping Danni or one of her parents might have seen him. She certainly wasn't expecting the sight that greeted her.

Mr Harris was standing behind the bakery's counter, breaking eggs into a bowl, with Louisa supervising him. He was wearing a Cake Hunters apron over his scruffy tweed jacket, a baker's hat, and a pair of black-rimmed glasses with fake eyes over the lenses to disguise his own large, singular eye. He had been wearing the same ones when Grace had first met him, in the Houses of Parliament. While Grace thought it was still startlingly obvious that he was, in fact, a massive great cyclops, the customers sitting at the back of the bakery must have been enjoying their pastries so much that they hadn't noticed.

'What's going on?' Grace whispered to Danni, who was putting strawberries on top of dainty-looking custard tarts.

Danni wiped her hands on her apron and leaned towards her little sister. 'He came down early when Mum and I were getting everything ready for opening time. He seemed so interested that Mum said he could help if he wanted to.'

'He'll explode again if we're not careful,' said Grace.

Danni shook her head. 'Don't worry about that. He has gloves on so he can't possibly touch any baking powder.'

Grace glanced at Mr Harris and saw that he was wearing yellow rubber gloves – the sort you wear when you put bleach down the toilet – on both hands. Despite their size, the rubber was

straining to contain his meaty hands.

'They were the only ones he could squeeze into,' said Danni.

'Wow,' said Grace, walking over to him. 'Good morning, Mr Harris.'

'Good day,' he replied, not looking up. 'You can hardly call this morning. You're a very lazy Doughnut Lady.'

'I was up late researching Bottom Biters,' Grace said quietly. She didn't want any of the customers to overhear her. 'Which is actually your job!'

The cyclops tutted. 'Stop crowding me. I am folding the eggs in.'

Grace rolled her eyes. 'What are you making?'

'A very complicated and precise recipe, so please leave me to concentrate,' he replied.

'He's making fairy cakes,' Louisa interjected. Grace giggled.

Mr Harris frowned. 'And, come to think of it, I haven't put in a single fairy yet,' he said. 'Have I missed a step?' He looked around. 'Do you use dried, fresh or pickled? I find all of them delicious. They have a certain umami.'

'Er, no,' said Louisa. 'No actual fairies in this recipe.'

'How odd,' said Mr Harris. 'And what a stupid name for cakes with no fairies in them.'

'And no baking powder either,' said Louisa to Grace. 'I decided not to include any at all –

you know, just in case. We don't want a scene in the bakery on a Saturday morning.'

Grace nodded. 'You can try them, Mr Harris, once we're back from Max and Frank's house.'

Mr Harris shook his head. 'I'm not going.'

'We both are,' said Grace. 'We have another monster-hunting exercise and we need to discuss this Bottom Biter.' She held up her notes. 'You start your new job on Monday – we'll be meeting the Head of the Secret Service! That's only two days away.'

'You can go. I'll stay here. I like this job better,' said Mr Harris, sniffing the cake mixture.

'Oh no, Mr Harris!' said Louisa, appearing slightly terrified at the prospect of a new, green employee. 'You must do your very important Secret Service job! Danni and I can keep showing you how to bake on your days off. You're only part-time, so you'll have plenty of opportunities.'

'Fine,' snapped the cyclops. 'But I may not be able to work

45

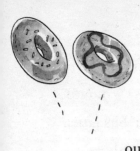 here on all of my days off, now I've had to postpone the trip I had planned to go on today, to help you out.'

'Where were you going today?' asked Grace.

'Mind your own business, Doughnut Lady,' the cyclops said tartly.

'While you live here, it's all of our business,' said Grace.

'Nosy,' muttered Mr Harris. 'Nosy bakery people.'

'Well, it doesn't matter anyway. Dad's going to drive us to the House by the River now,' Grace said cheerily.

'I want to try my cakes!' he wailed.

'I'll save you some,' said Louisa. 'You can take something else to eat with you, if you like.'

'Oh!' said the cyclops, brightening up. 'I'll have this.' He pointed to a wedding cake in the window.

'Not that one,' said Grace.

'This one,' said Mr Harris, pointing to a towering chocolate cake behind the counter. Grace shook her head. He poked a big green finger into the icing and swirled it round.

'Mr Harris!' said Grace in disbelief.

'Oops,' he said. 'My finger slipped. You can't sell it now.'

'Take the cake,' Louisa said, defeated. She handed over a tall white cake box.

'How kind – thank you,' Mr Harris said, scooping the cake up in one hand and dropping it, upside down, into the box. 'Okay, Doughnut Lady, if you insist I have to come with you because you can't do anything on your own, then I'm ready.' He marched off towards the door, still wearing his apron and hat.

CHAPTER SEVEN

Mr Harris Eats the Evidence

Grace, Frank, Max and Eamon sat round the meeting table in the cellar of the House by the River, while Mr Harris wandered round, poking, sniffing and, once, licking things of interest. Grace explained what she had found out about Bottom Biters, and Frank occasionally chipped in with his own research.

'The one we are looking for seems to be quite rare,' Grace said. 'Not many of them cause a rash with their bites. And Bottom Biters are one of the few monsters that can't be destroyed with just baking powder. The best way to get rid of them is with a garlic and herb savoury muffin applied directly to the mouth and fangs, as well as exposing them to a form of natural light. But doing all of that can be difficult because they're very fighty.'

Frank nodded. 'They are. They also have an excellent s-sense of smell and taste, which means most of them are very interested in food and drink. This one seems to really like human products.'

'Which explains it stealing from shops here in our world,' said Eamon.

'But not so much the biting of bottoms,' Max said. From across the room, Mr Harris chuckled.

'It's a character trait of this type of m-monster,' Frank explained. 'They just can't stop themselves biting things.'

'I assume it's using a Monster World gateway to get here?' asked Eamon.

'It has to be,' said Grace. 'But they're one-way, so we don't know how it's getting back *to* Monster World.'

'I've heard there are gateways that go to Monster World here in London,' said Frank.

Mr Harris plodded over to the table, suddenly looking interested. 'Where?' he demanded. 'I've always had to explode to get back to Monster World, which is very unfair!'

'I've been through one,' said Max. 'But I had been kidnapped by an incredibly rare and large Freak-footed Troll and was inside his suitcase, so I never got to see where it was. Horribly uncomfortable, that was. But it did result in me finding Frank, so it was worth the muscle cramp. Other than that, we were never able to find one in all the years we were out in the field.'

Eamon frowned and nodded in agreement.

'Well, it seems like our bottom-biting target might have,' said Grace. 'So, I guess if we find the gateway, we find the Bottom Biter.'

Max nodded. 'And talking about finding things leads us perfectly into Mr Harris's next

exercise. Frank, would you like to explain?'

Frank nodded and looked nervously at the cyclops. 'There are three c-common monsters in our garden, all hiding in places they like to live. You have ten minutes to find and secure all three of them. You're looking for a Poo Shuffler, a Vegetable Nibbler and a Tripper Upper. And, Mr Harris? Please t-t-try not to eat any of them.'

'A Poo Nibbler, a Vegetable Shuffler and a what?' snapped Mr Harris. 'These all sound like small-fry monsters.'

'Well then, you should have no problem dealing with them,' said Grace. 'Especially if you've read the notes I gave you.'

'I don't need notes,' said the cyclops testily. 'Come on, Doughnut Lady, let's get this over and done with.'

'I'm not helping. I'll be watching. You have to do this on your own. If you get into trouble, we can have a code word for you to shout. What about

doughnuts?' said Grace, smiling. Mr Harris could never resist a doughnut.

'Ooh, yum! Doughnuts!' he shouted. Then he glared at her. 'Hang on. What difficulty could *I* possibly get into? I won't be shouting anything.'

Seventeen minutes later, Mr Harris had eaten all three monsters during what could only be described as a chaotic and – at times – terrifying training exercise. He was dangling an unexpected fourth monster above his enormous mouth when Grace shouted, 'Stop!'

Mr Harris dropped the tiny, squirming, thread-like creature into his mouth and widened his eye, as if he had no idea what she was talking about.

'Spit him out NOW!' Grace yelled at Mr Harris. 'I saw what you did! That's a tiny, harmless Key Catcher. Don't you dare eat it!'

'I don't know what you're talking about,

Doughnut Lady,' mumbled Mr Harris with his mouth half closed. 'Why would I eat anything as titchy and stringy as a Key Catcher? I'm sure it'd have no nutritional value whatso –'

The cyclops was interrupted by the tiny monster emerging from the gap between his lips on one side. It launched itself out with surprising force for something so small and wiry, and rocketed into the air.

Grace vaulted forward and caught it neatly. The little creature curled itself round her index finger and blew her endless kisses in thanks.

'You failed the mission and ate an innocent bystander!' hissed Grace.

'It was an accident. I saw him on the potting shed padlock and thought he was trying to break in. I went above and beyond the call of duty,' said Mr Harris curtly. 'And I didn't fail the mission. I think you'll find that all three target monsters are gone.'

'You took almost twice as long as you should have and you've digested the evidence. Again!' Grace said, shaking her head in disbelief.

'Stop making a fuss,' said Mr Harris flatly. 'Shrimp Boy, how did you rate my performance?'

Frank was standing very close to Max, his fork clenched so tightly in his hand, his knuckles were white.

'Okay, in the circumstances,' he whispered.

'There you are,' said Mr Harris,

pointing a sausage-like finger in Frank's direction. 'Even that puny weakling speaks more sense than you do.'

'Perhaps it's time to call it a day?' said Eamon. 'Why don't we go back to the bakery and prepare for our meeting with the Colonel first thing on Monday? You need to keep in mind that Colonel Patience Hardy spent twenty years as a Commando in the Royal Marines before becoming Head of the Secret Service – she's quite the opposite of what her first name suggests. It's best we arrive having done as much research as possible.'

'Yes, Doughnut Lady's dad!' Mr Harris cheered. 'Let's go back and prepare . . . or not bother! It must be time for me to try my no-fairy, stupidly named fairy cakes! At last!'

'I'm not sure you deserve any,' said Grace, looking at the little Key Catcher still in her hand.

'You need to get over it,' Mr Harris replied. 'Put it down so we can go home to eat cake.'

'You mean to prepare for our meeting?' said Grace, putting her hand down to the floor to let the Key Catcher go. But it ran further up her arm.

'Do you want to come with us?' she asked. It nodded enthusiastically, patting her sleeve.

'It can't come back to *our* bakery!' cried Mr Harris. 'It's a common monster. It'll be locking things and hiding keys all over the place!'

Grace stared at him. 'Of course it can come back with us. Key Catchers make excellent companions and I'd like this one to be mine.'

The tiny creature jumped up and down, punching the air.

Mr Harris narrowed his eye. 'Fine,' he spat. 'But don't think for a single minute that it's having any of my fairy cakes.'

CHAPTER EIGHT

A Fairy Big Explosion

'These are the best no-fairy fairy cakes I have ever had!' Mr Harris declared triumphantly, shoving the last five of his cakes, paper cases still attached, into his giant mouth at once.

'Annoyingly, it seems like you're a lot better at baking than you are at monster-hunting,' said Grace, taking in the cyclops's smug expression.

Mr Harris ignored her and turned to Louisa. 'May I take this to read before I sleep?' he said, holding up a recipe book from a shelf behind the counter. It was entitled *Complex Patisserie for Master Bakers*.

Louisa nodded. 'Yes, of course. It's quite advanced though, Mr Harris.'

'Not a problem,' he said confidently. 'I'm clearly a natural, so I doubt it'll take me long to get to this standard.'

Grace and Danni tried to cover their giggles but failed miserably. The cyclops glared at them, before clamping the book under his arm and making his way upstairs.

Half an hour later, Grace climbed the stairs with the rescued Key Catcher on her shoulder. He showed no sign of wanting to leave her side. She headed to the study in the attic to fetch a research book that she wanted to read.

'That's odd,' she said. The study door was open and the Monster Scanner on. 'I'm sure I shut the door and turned the Monster Scanner off.'

The tiny monster scratched its head in confusion.

Grace walked over to the computer and inspected the screen. It was blank, except for the search field at the top. Next to the magnifying glass icon was a single 'G'.

'I wonder if Dad was using it?' she mumbled. She made a mental note to ask him in the morning, then turned her head to address the Key Catcher, who had slid down her arm and was sitting astride the computer's mouse. 'While we're here, would you mind if I found out a bit more about you? Could you type your name in? Or I could use our new scanner to scan you.'

The thread-like monster jumped up and down in excitement and made a swooshing motion with its arm.

'Scan you?' asked Grace.

It nodded enthusiastically.

Grace picked up a device that looked like a supermarket barcode scanner. 'I haven't used this yet but, don't worry, it should only take a few seconds and you won't feel a thing.'

The Key Catcher stood perfectly still, as if it was made of stone, its arms outstretched and feet apart. Grace scanned him quickly. The Monster Scanner's screen burst into life immediately.

Name: Kenneth Arthur Locke (likes to be known as Kenny)
Type: Key Catcher
Age: 8 years
Height: 6 cm

Weight: Under 1g

Strengths: 10 detected: kindness, flexibility, affection, willingness to help, loyalty, strength, unlocking things, speed, resilience, dedication to a cause.

Weaknesses: 1 detected: naivety.

Likes: Locks, yoga, traditional wooden puzzles, cryptic crosswords, cute animals, helping others, limbo dancing.

Dislikes: Almost nothing.

Best form of destruction: Should not be destroyed. The most helpful and loyal monster species by far.

Notes: Key Catchers can be mischievous. Nine times out of ten, when your key gets stuck in a lock, it's because a Key Catcher is hanging on to it for fun. They are unbelievably strong for their size. They make excellent companions.

SCORING:

Friendship: 100

Size: 2

Courage: 95

Kindness: 100

Intelligence: 85

Loyalty: 100

Violence: 0

Danger: 0

Type: Fairly common.

Location: Cake Hunters, Camden

'So your name's Kenny?' said Grace.

The Key Catcher nodded happily and took a bow.

'And you're sticking with me, are you?' she asked, smiling. He nodded again, eagerly.

She closed down the Monster Scanner and held her hand out for Kenny to climb onto. She glanced over the landing at the door to Mr Harris's room. Then she looked back at the

Monster Scanner and shut the study door.

'Kenny, would you be able to lock the study door, please?' she said very quietly.

Kenny saluted and launched himself off her hand. He swooped neatly into the lock. *Clunk*.

Grace was woken by a rustling noise coming from downstairs. According to her clock, it was just after three a.m. Kenny was still curled up, fast asleep in the yellow spotty fairy cake case he was using as a bed. Soundlessly, she crept out from under her duvet and crossed her room, snatching a pot of baking powder from the top of her chest of drawers as she went. It wouldn't be the first time she had come across a pilfering Pie Pincher or a sneaky Snack Snaffler in the middle of the night.

Grace inched down the stairs until she reached the door that led into the bakery. She paused, then shoved it open suddenly, hoping to surprise whoever, or whatever, was in there.

'Oh! Mr Harris!' she exclaimed. 'What on earth are you doing?'

The cyclops turned round slowly. He had a baking tray full of fairy cakes in one hand and an empty tray in the other.

'Doughnut Lady!' he bellowed. Crumbs sprayed out of his mouth. 'For goodness' sake, you made me jump.'

'Have you eaten all those cakes?' she demanded.

Mr Harris glanced down at the empty tray and whipped it behind his back. 'No! I was just going to eat these – the ones I made. That cake book made me snacky.' He tipped the full tray into his gullet.

'But Mr Harris –' started Grace.

'Oh, here we go,' interrupted the cyclops, mouth full. '*You've* eaten all the cakes, Mr Harris . . . even though *you* made them . . . and therefore you're perfectly *entitled* to eat them . . . and . . . oh.' He paused and frowned. 'My tummy feels funny. Why does my tummy feel funny? Are you trying to explode me again, Doughnut Lady? I thought we were over that.'

'No! You're trying to explode yourself!' cried Grace. 'They weren't the fairy cakes you made – you ate all of those earlier. Those were another batch Danni made. With baking powder in! Mr Harris, what have you done?'

Before she could finish, the cyclops went very still and mumbled a very quiet, 'Oh no . . .'

The door from upstairs opened again and Louisa, Eamon and Danni burst into the room.

Mr Harris gave a little wave. And exploded.

CHAPTER NINE

Bitey Joe's

'Stupid but brilliant, that's what I am,' hissed Mr Harris as he landed, with a violent jolt, on a particularly pointy cobble in Monster World. 'If I wasn't such a brilliant baker, I wouldn't have been so stupid as to eat all those cakes,' he carried on muttering. 'I have suffered for my gift. And now . . . my bottom hurts.' He pulled himself to his feet and looked round. He was standing by a fast food restaurant called Burger Thing.

The owner, a very fat and shiny Grease Gobbler, was throwing two trolls out of the door. 'You can't pay me with fake magic beans, you thieving scoundrels!' he yelled as they scurried off. 'Why are trolls so cheap?!' He slammed the door.

Mr Harris nodded in agreement. 'They are cheap.' Now he'd seen where he was, he was much happier. He remembered that Burger Thing was next door to Cookie Monsters, the bakery where Eamon and Louisa had worked when they lived in Monster World, after he had eaten them a couple of years before. And that was useful, because Mr Harris also knew that there were two gateways back to Human World just metres away.

'I might have time for a snack,' he said to himself, rubbing his ginormous stomach. 'They had very good doughnuts here.'

The bakery window display, however, seemed to have gone downhill. A pile of mouldy avocados sat limply at the back next to a half-eaten prawn and lettuce sandwich. Some shrivelled Cornish pasties dangled upside down from the top of the window, like bats. A marrow had been plonked near the glass and 'decorated' with what looked like tortilla chips. Bananas were mashed against the glass in a gooey, grey mess. It was complete chaos.

'What is this?' said Mr Harris in disbelief. He stepped back to look at the sign. 'Bitey Joe's,' he read out loud. 'What's Bitey Joe's?'

He pushed open the door to investigate what had happened to the once wonderful bakery, only to find it was locked. A sign had been hastily written in red, drippy ink:

WE ARE CLOSED. BUT COME BACK WHEN WE ARE OPEN – EVERY DAY

(FROM MIDNIGHT TO 4.30 A.M. IN SUMMER AND FROM 11 P.M. TO 6 A.M. IN WINTER)

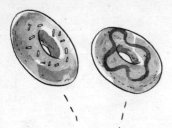

As Mr Harris scowled at the ridiculous opening times, he heard a wail behind him. He turned round. A tall monster with a large red nose, skinny legs and a pot belly stood behind him. He had one hand against his forehead, one on his hip, another (which was holding a dripping ice-cream cone) gesticulated wildly in the air, and the last pointed desperately to Bitey Joe's. He was cursing quietly in Italian.

'Wow, a real Gelato Guzzler,' Mr Harris mumbled. 'Must go, or I'll be here all day listening to his life story.' He began to move away.

'Dis!' came a cry in a thick Italian accent. 'Dis was my drrream!'

'Oh dear,' sneered Mr Harris. 'Better look for a new one.'

'No, no, no . . . you don't understand,' said the Gelato Guzzler sadly. 'I would 'ave made dis place wonderrrful! I am Marietto Monta in Gondola, rrrenowned Monster Worrrld ice crrream specialist!' He spread his four arms wide and bowed extravagantly.

'Who?' Mr Harris said grumpily. 'Never heard of you. Anyway, what sort of name is that?'

'MARRRIETTO Monta in Gondola!' the Gelato Guzzler repeated. 'It means "Little Mario in a boat". I came to Monster World in a boat from Italy so it makes perrrfect sense! I am a rrrrenowned Monster Worrrld gelato crrreator. It was my drrream to turn dis place into an ice crrream parrrlourrr to die for!' A small sob escaped his throat.

'Well, take it over then,' snapped Mr Harris. 'It's hideous now so you can't make it any worse.' He started to stomp away.

Marietto called after him. 'But I can't! No one can! Bitey Joe is fearrrrsome and bad. 'E would bite my bottom – or, worse still, my 'ands!'

Mr Harris stopped in his tracks, recalling his case and the conversation at Max's house. 'He'd bite your what?'

Marietto twisted his lower half round and gestured to his bottom with all four hands. 'Dis! My *bellissimo* bottom! 'E is a Bottom Biter, after all!'

Mr Harris looked quizzically at Marietto. 'A Bottom Biter, you say? How much do you know about him?'

Marietto leaned in, checking to see if anyone was nearby. 'I know a lot, my frrrriend,' he whispered. 'Come back to my house and I will explain. You can be de first to try my new gelato flavourrr. It is made from de bogeys of Snot-nosed Ogres. Delicious!'

CHAPTER TEN

Just in Time

Mr Harris arrived back at the bakery with a bunch of breadsticks and a recipe for Italian ice-cream cake poking out of his jacket pocket. He clutched a folded-up sketch of Bitey Joe that Marietto had drawn for him.

He opened the door and the bell jangled.

'Oh, Mr Harris!' said Danni, looking up from her mixing bowl. 'You're back.'

'Yes. Please let Doughnut Lady know. I'm going for a nap,' he replied, striding towards the door marked *Private*.

'She's not here,' said Danni. 'They've all gone. They waited as long as they could for you but the meeting starts in ten minutes.'

The cyclops stopped and turned to Danni. 'Which meeting?'

'The one with the Head of the Secret Service,' she replied. 'You've been gone more than twenty-four hours, Mr Harris. If you leave now, you might only be a few minutes late.'

Mr Harris arrived at Colonel Hardy's office just as Grace, Frank, Eamon and Max were called in.

'Where've you been?' growled Grace as Mr Harris walked in casually behind her.

'On an information-gathering mission,' he snapped. 'Some of us have been working hard.'

'You exploded yourself because you ate all the cakes! You weren't on a mission!' she whispered. From Grace's pocket, Kenny shook his head in disbelief.

'Yes, I was, and that's what I shall tell the Colonel,' he said matter-of-factly.

The office was sleek and minimal, and decorated in black, white and grey. It was just down the corridor from Prime Minister Attwood's office. Grace shuddered at the thought of being inside it with Mr Harris's murderous, shape-shifting grandfather, Neville. Luckily, they had managed to explode him just before he tried to take over the country with an army of evil monsters. All in a monster-hunting day's work.

Colonel Patience Hardy sat behind her shiny desk, which was entirely empty. She wore a sharp black suit jacket and a pristine white shirt. Her black hair was pulled back into a perfect, tight bun and her dark skin was flawless. She watched them enter one by one before barking at them. 'Sit!'

Everyone, even Mr Harris, sat down quicker than if they had been playing a

fiercely competitive game of musical chairs.

She glanced at her watch. 'I have just less than thirteen minutes to hear what you have to say, so let's make this snappy. First, you.' She pointed at Mr Harris. 'How is your training progressing?'

'I have excelled in all areas, Mrs Not-Very-Patient,' replied the cyclops.

Grace bit her tongue and exchanged a look with Frank, while Kenny peeked out of the top of Grace's pocket, looking shocked.

'Please address me correctly, Mr Harris,' said Colonel Hardy. 'Either Mr Hunter, is this true?' She gestured towards Max and Eamon.

Max cleared his throat. 'There's still a way to go, ma'am, but we'll make sure we're on hand to help Mr Harris in these first few weeks.'

Mr Harris whipped round to Max. 'Excuse me? There will be no need for you to be *on hand*.

You weren't *on hand* when I risked my life just yesterday to find out information about that ridiculous Bottom Biter.'

'No interrupting!' snapped Colonel Hardy. 'We're down to twelve minutes and counting. Tell me what information you found out about the target monster, and how you found it.'

'Well, I found it because I am diligent and expeditious,' Mr Harris replied smugly.

Grace wasn't completely sure what either word meant but suspected Mr Harris was neither of them. She bit her tongue even harder.

Colonel Hardy leaned forward over her desk. 'I will decide if you are either of those things, Mr Harris. All I want to hear is the information relevant to the case.'

Mr Harris frowned. 'No need to have a tantrum,' he muttered. Seeing the Colonel's nostrils flare, he quickly continued, 'The Bottom Biter you're looking for goes by the name of Bitey Joe. He is working out of the bakery previously named Cookie Monsters in Monster World.'

'Ma'am, excuse me for interrupting, but Cookie Monsters was where Louisa and I lived when we were in Monster World!' exclaimed Eamon.

'Shhh,' scolded Mr Harris. 'No interrupting – she's told us once already. Now, the bakery has been unimaginatively renamed Bitey Joe's. I am also working, expeditiously, to find the gateway Bitey Joe is using to return to Monster World but, so far, that remains unidentified.'

Colonel Hardy frowned. Quickly Mr Harris continued, 'I also diligently acquired this valuable piece of evidence.' He pulled Marietto's sketch from his pocket.

'Show me,' Colonel Hardy demanded.

'Certainly, Your Highness,' said Mr Harris, shooting Grace a self-important look. He shuffled

over to the desk and handed the Colonel the
scrappy piece of paper.

She held it up. Then twisted it round so it was
the opposite way up. 'Is this a joke?'

Mr Harris shook his head. 'Absolutely not.

This is a top-quality, artistic interpretation direct from Monster World. Although I haven't actually studied it yet myself.'

Colonel Hardy turned the piece of paper round so he could see it. A quiet groan came from Max's direction.

'It appears to have been sketched by a five-year-old, Mr Harris,' Colonel Hardy said.

The scrawled drawing showed a tall, thin stick man with an enormous head. Marietto had drawn two dots for eyes, a V-shape for a nose and a wide mouth with what looked like two pointy fangs. Over the top of the stick body, he had scribbled a long triangle, so it appeared that Bitey Joe was wearing either a dress or a cloak. He had printed *I hate you, Bitey Joe!* underneath the picture.

'Stupid Gelato Guzzler,' Mr Harris hissed under his breath. 'Can't draw for toffee. You'd think having four hands would make him a better artist.'

A timid voice came from somewhere behind the cyclops.

'C-Colonel Hardy,' said Frank, 'I know it's not a very good drawing, but the Monster Scanner should be able to pick up details we can't see ourselves.'

Colonel Hardy raised her perfectly shaped eyebrows. 'Let's hope so. You can sit down now, Mr Harris. Please take this with you.' She wafted the drawing in the air dismissively. 'Find out what you can and report back. In the last twenty-four hours, there have been another two bitings. Unfortunately, one of the people bitten was Prime Minister Attwood's husband, Norman.'

She held up a newspaper. The dramatic headline on the front page read:

PM'S HUSBAND, NORMAN, SUSTAINS INJURIES IN VICIOUS ATTACK THAT HAS LEFT HIM UNABLE TO SIT DOWN!

Mr Harris chuckled behind his enormous hand.

'Something funny, Mr Harris?' Colonel Hardy demanded.

'Norman!' he spluttered. 'It's a funny name.'

She glared at him. 'Find the beast responsible,' she said firmly. 'Now, we have just two minutes left. Has there been any progress on the disappearance of the television show judge?'

Mr Harris looked flustered. 'No. And honestly, Patient Lady Ma'am, I don't think there's any point looking for him. He is obviously fed up of the fame and attention. Let's leave him in peace, I say. Case closed . . .'

'Actually, I have a lead, Colonel,' Frank said timidly. 'I'm just waiting for the CCTV footage from the London Palladium, where he was last seen. I'll review it and send you a report.'

Mr Harris whipped his head round towards Frank. Forgetting the

no-interruption rule, he snapped, 'I will review it. It's *my* case, Shrimp Boy.'

'Mr Harris!' said Colonel Hardy. 'Please discuss who is doing what outside this meeting. We have one minute and twenty seconds left, and I'd like to finish early.'

'Fine,' said Mr Harris pointedly. 'I was just saying I can do it. I am diligent and expeditious.'

'That will be all,' said Colonel Hardy. 'Dismissed.'

'Well, she's a piece of work. Very rude,' said Mr Harris as they walked away from Colonel Hardy's office.

'How did you find all of that information out? You're not making it up, are you?' Grace asked.

The cyclops shook his head in disbelief. 'You're very rude too. You could just say "Thank you, Mr Harris. You're very good at your job, Mr Harris. You're diligent and –"'

'Expeditious!' finished Grace. 'Now please tell me how you got the information.'

'If you must know, I have an undercover source,' said Mr Harris. 'He's very reliable. And not at all crazy.'

Grace frowned, unconvinced. 'Well, there's one very easy way to find out if you're lying,' she said.

'M-Monster Scanner?' suggested Frank.

'Bingo,' she said. 'Let's go back to the bakery and see what we can find out about Bitey Joe.'

CHAPTER ELEVEN

No Ordinary Bottom Biter

Grace, Frank, Kenny and Mr Harris crowded round the Monster Scanner as it conjured up the information they were looking for.

Name: Joseph Von Toothenmeister,

a.k.a. Bitey Joe

Type: Bottom Biter (see notes)

Age: 104 years

Height: 183 cm

Weight: 160 lb

Strengths: 8 detected: fangs, speed, stealth, gliding/swooping (but only for short distances), operating in darkness, super-human strength, hearing, never gets old.

Weaknesses: 3 detected: concentrated beams of natural light, garlic, stakes (wooden).

Likes: Steaks (meaty), sunglasses, roller-coasters, caramel, night-time, dentists, being scary, castles, BBQs, biting things, flossing and good dental hygiene.

Dislikes: Tropical holidays, conservatories, soup, tofu, vegans, dancing, breakfast tele-vision, garlic bread.

Best form of destruction: A garlic and herb muffin (with lashings of baking powder) applied directly to the fangs, preferably while in direct sunlight or in a beam of moonlight from a full moon.

Notes: This Bottom Biter is a fearsome cross between a mutant vampire bat and Shadow Stalker. Victims of his bottom-biting may display some strange behaviour, as well as an unsightly purple rash. Treat with extreme caution (and lots of garlic) at all times.

SCORING:

Friendship: 0

Size: 81

Courage: 92

Kindness: 1

Intelligence: 77

Loyalty: 4

Violence: 84

Danger: 98

Type: RARE.

Location: Monster World

While Grace read the information, Kenny sat on her shoulder and plaited three of her hairs.

'Frank, this isn't good. Bitey Joe isn't a normal Bottom Biter; he's a really dangerous one. He's part mutant vampire bat – not just any old vampire bat!'

'He's not dangerous,' said Mr Harris dismissively. 'I know that because of my under-cover mission to Monster World.'

'Undercover mission? More like accidental mission!' Grace laughed as she turned to Frank. 'We need to find out how Bitey Joe is getting back to Monster World. If there's a hidden gateway in London, we need to find it.'

Frank tapped the Monster Scanner keyboard and printed a map with a series of red and green dots scattered over it. 'I looked at all the information we had and put this together,' he said, pointing with his fork. 'The red dots show the locations where people have had their bottoms bitten, and the green dots show all the food thefts. They were probably carried out by the same monster. There's a list of people and shops on the next page.'

'This is brilliant!' exclaimed Grace, studying the map. From the desk, Kenny beamed at Frank and punched the air in admiration.

Mr Harris tutted loudly. 'All reports and no action,' he said.

'We need to work out a plan using the

information we have,' said Grace, not taking her eyes away from the print-out. Kenny nodded. Mr Harris glared at him.

'You need to ask questions, hide in a car and take photos, and carry out house-to-house enquiries,' said Mr Harris knowledgeably.

'You've watched too many police programmes,' said Grace. 'Monster-hunting is different.'

Mr Harris snorted rudely. 'Says the human

child to the very important cyclops. I think I know more than you do!'

Kenny shook his head and pointed at Grace, implying she knew more than anyone. Behind Grace, Mr Harris reached forward and grabbed Kenny between his thumb and forefinger and dangled him over his cavernous mouth. Kenny put his hands together in a prayer position and closed his eyes.

'Put. Him. Down,' said Grace, her eyes still on the screen.

Mr Harris scowled and flicked Kenny back onto the desk. The little Key Catcher landed smoothly with a James Bond-like forward roll and scurried up Grace's shoulder to hide in her hair.

'Frank, look,' she said, pointing to the map. 'All the attacks have happened in the South Kensington area.'

 90

'I noticed that,' said Frank. 'Lots of tourists to bite, I suppose.'

'Exactly, and lots of places to take food from,' said Grace.

'South Kensington?' said Mr Harris. 'I know that place. Is that where you can ice skate outside at Christmas? A very rude man once said he would not ice skate at the same time as me because I was too big and would probably crack the ice.'

'Yes, outside the museum. And, you're right, that was very rude,' said Grace.

Mr Harris nodded. 'It turned out fine, though. I ate him.'

'What?' cried Grace.

Mr Harris rolled his eye. 'Don't worry, he skated first. I'm not unreasonable.'

'Oh my goblins,' Frank whispered. Kenny climbed into Grace's right ear, for safety. She was about to ask Mr Harris not to talk about his previous people-eaty actions when the cyclops began to jump up and down with glee. The family portraits on the wall above the fireplace started to shake and a number of books fell off the mantelpiece.

'The museum!' he exclaimed. 'I almost forgot – it's the one with the dinosaurs! Monsters LOVE going there. There are always loads of the annoying small humans that get under your feet.'

Grace looked at Frank. 'What if there's a reason for that? What if the gateway to Monster World is in the Natural History Museum?' she said slowly. 'We need to see for ourselves, and there's no reason to wait. Let's go now.'

CHAPTER TWELVE

The Museum

Grace, Frank, Kenny, Max, Eamon and a very grumpy cyclops disguised (badly) as a human arrived outside the imposing Natural History Museum half an hour later. Mr Harris had grumbled for the entire journey about the short-notice visit ruining his chance to make shortbread with Danni at Cake Hunters.

'Perfect shortbread is a form of art,' he moaned. 'You've ruined my day.'

'You said you love the museum!' exclaimed Grace. 'And shortbread is easy. I can show you how to make it when we're back.'

The cyclops snorted rudely. 'As if *you* could do it. You wouldn't know how to make the texture a perfect crumbly consistency that melts onto the palate.'

'You wouldn't know if it was crumbly or melty!' laughed Grace. 'You don't even chew your food.'

'I'd chew you,' Mr Harris mumbled as Eamon and Max led the way up the stone steps to the entrance.

The museum's entrance hall was vast and grand. An enormous stone staircase dominated one end of the room and striking arched alcoves lined the sides. Before they had walked twenty steps, a Snack Snaffler shot past them, holding a fruit pastille aloft in one of its big hairy hands.

'Didn't take long,' Eamon commented, watching it dodge people and pushchairs as it sprinted towards its chosen hiding place.

'Look,' said Frank quietly, 'is that a Trinket Trader? I've never seen one in real life.' He pointed to a mole-like creature wearing a trilby hat. It was pressed up against the wall, camouflaged, next to a glass display of ancient pottery. It had a bag in one hand and a kind of hand-held grabber in the other.

Max nodded. 'It's up to no good. Mr Harris, you could try to catch or explode that Trinket Trader. It would be good on-the-job training and it might stop a theft.'

Mr Harris rolled his eye under his fake two-eye glasses. 'Fine,' he snapped. 'Wait here.' Then he stomped away – in the opposite direction to the Trinket Trader.

The cyclops returned a couple of minutes later with a paper bag from the museum café. He walked straight past Grace, Frank, Kenny, Eamon and Max without acknowledging them, and went over to the Trinket Trader.

'Oh no,' breathed Grace. 'What's he doing?' She watched as Mr Harris got closer to the creature. It noticed him straight away – he was about as subtle as a wildebeest. But before the monster could make a run for it, Mr Harris thrust his hand inside the bag, pulled out a sizeable fruit scone and lobbed it at the Trinket Trader's head. The boulder-like scone hit its target full on, sending the Trinket Trader spiralling across the shiny floor and under the glass display cabinet, where it came to a halt and lay, unconscious.

Grace skidded over. 'What was that?' she asked in disbelief.

'Why hasn't it exploded?' Mr Harris poked it with his shoe.

'It won't explode with a normal scone! You need one with too much baking powder, or whatever is best to destroy Trinket Traders. You've just knocked it out,' she said.

'Excellent,' said Mr Harris, picking it up by one leg so its hat dropped to the floor, revealing a bald, shiny head. 'It will squirm less.' He turned his head away and, before Grace could stop him, dropped the creature into his mouth. Kenny covered his eyes in horror and hid in Grace's pocket.

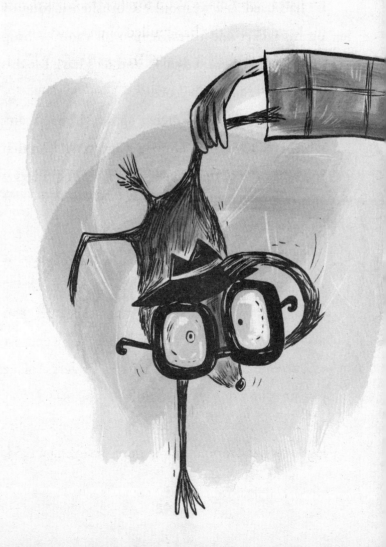

'He's eaten it, hasn't he?' asked Max as he reached Grace. She nodded.

'No one saw. Job done,' said the cyclops, bending down and picking up the fruit scone he had used as a weapon. He brushed it roughly on his jacket and threw it into his mouth. 'Stop giving me unplanned tasks and let's look for this gateway.' He marched off.

As the group hurried after him, Frank whispered to Grace, 'Do you want to tell him that the best cake of destruction for Trinket Traders is shortbread, or shall I?'

CHAPTER THIRTEEN

The Gateway

Grace had barely set foot in the Blue Zone of the museum when a Tripper Upper ran past her, shooting its leg out and making her stumble into the back of Mr Harris.

'Calm down, Doughnut Lady, you don't always have to be first,' he snapped. 'Right, where do you want to go? Dinosaurs, mammals or marine invertebrates?'

Kenny jumped up and down on Grace's shoulder and pointed towards the dinosaur area.

'Let's go to the dinosaurs first,' said Grace.

'What, because that stick insect has a hunch?' hissed Mr Harris, glaring at the Key Catcher.

'I don't think it's a hunch,' said Frank. 'Look.'

Among the people filing into the dinosaur area, Grace saw a Hair Knotter hanging from a little girl's ponytail. It was tying all the loose strands in tight knots. Then she spotted two

YEE HAW!

Button Gobblers scurrying between people's feet, stopping occasionally to pick up a fallen coat button (or to chew a perfectly good one off someone's jacket). High above her head, she caught sight of a Dust Popper, leaping from light to light, merrily farting out dust as it went.

'There's loads of monster activity here,' said Grace, taking her rucksack off her shoulders and reaching inside for her camera and notebook.

As they filed towards the main attraction, an animatronic T-Rex that moved and roared, Grace noticed movement behind the curtain that was the backdrop for the ferocious-looking dinosaur. 'Look over there,' she said quietly. Then she said to Mr Harris. 'Don't make it obvious!'

'I'll just go and have a proper look. Let's not dilly dally,' said Mr Harris impatiently.

'No!' said Grace. 'Everyone will see you. We need to do this carefully so no one sees.'

Kenny tugged on her ear lobe and pointed to himself.

'Do you want to go and look, Kenny?' asked Grace.

The tiny creature nodded, barely able to contain his excitement.

'Perfect,' said Eamon. 'There's no chance anyone will notice you.'

Mr Harris moaned under his breath as the Key Catcher jumped up and down in excitement, saluted like an army major then leapt majestically into the air. The moment he left her shoulder, Grace could no longer see him. She hoped he could dodge all the stampy feet, although she knew that, even if he didn't, he would be fine. Key Catchers were the most flexible, resilient monsters she had ever come across. It was as though they were made of fishing wire.

Two minutes later, Grace felt a tickle on her forearm. Kenny was back and bursting with excitement. He skipped from one spindly foot to the other, pointing in the direction he had come from.

'You found something!' said Grace.

Kenny nodded vigorously, jabbing his arms towards the curtain. The he stopped and mimed reaching down and pulling something up, trying to explain what he had seen.

'A ladder?' suggested Max.

Kenny shook his head.

'A gate?' asked Frank.

Kenny shook his head even faster, again miming pulling something up from by his feet.

'A trapdoor?' Grace ventured.

Kenny raised his arms in triumph.

'We need to see,' said Grace.

'We'll hang back and wait for it to quieten down,' replied Max.

'What a waste of time,' said Mr Harris, grumpily. 'It won't be anything.'

'We really should check, Mr Harris,' said Grace. 'Don't be a Negative Nora.'

The cyclops looked thunderous.

When almost all the other visitors in the dinosaur
area had moved on, Grace, with Kenny back on
her shoulder, Frank, Eamon, Max and Mr Harris
made their way over to the side of the exhibition.
One by one, they sneaked behind the curtain.

'There!' exclaimed Grace, pointing at a wooden trapdoor in the floor. It had a sign on it: DO NOT OPEN.

'Isn't it just part of the lighting system for the T-Rex?' questioned Max.

Mr Harris elbowed his way through and bent down, sniffing. 'Brussels sprouts . . . dust . . . rotten eggs . . .' he mumbled. 'Mouldy cheese! MONSTER WORLD!'

He wrenched off the sign, revealing a cast-iron handle underneath, flat to the surface of the trapdoor. He grabbed it and pulled.

CHAPTER FOURTEEN

Monster World

The trapdoor revealed a rickety-looking ladder. The rungs were uneven and appeared to be made out of a variety of objects – candy canes, umbrellas, golf clubs, bones, even what looked like a baguette.

'Well, that is useful to know,' said Mr Harris slamming the trapdoor shut. 'Right, let's go back to the bakery. I want to sample the shortbread I wasn't allowed to make, and I am also in charge of dessert this evening.'

'But we have to go down there!' said Grace. 'We've found the gateway to Monster World – this is massive!'

Max spoke up. 'There's no time like
the present, Mr Harris, and this is an
extraordinary discovery.'

Frank nodded and held up his fork, ready,
while Kenny enthusiastically did lunges on
Grace's shoulder in preparation.

'So I don't even get a say?' snapped Mr Harris.
'So much for Monster Rights!'

'Mr Harris,' said Grace, taking a deep breath,
'this won't take long. Before you know it, you'll
be eating biscuits and making dessert. We need
you to help. You know Monster World better
than the rest of us.'

Mr Harris pursed his lips then said, 'Fine. I
don't want your incompetence to reflect badly on
me so I have no choice but to come with you. I'm
taking no responsibility should you get eaten,
though.'

'Fair enough. Let's go!' cried Grace, approaching
the trapdoor.

'Slow down, Doughnut Lady!'

barked Mr Harris. 'What if there's a gatekeeping troll at the bottom? What are you going to do? Eat it? Move! Me first.' With that, he heaved himself onto the top of the ladder and disappeared down it surprisingly nimbly. Grace had only put one foot on the first rung of the ladder when a shout came from below.

'There was a troll! It has been . . . dealt with. Oh, and be careful on the second to last step. It's gone. It was a Toblerone. Delicious!'

'For goodness' sake, he's eaten the troll already,' said Grace, finding her footing and beginning to make her way down.

Frank, who was quivering, came next, his fork in his hand, then Max and lastly Eamon, who carefully closed the trapdoor above his head.

The ladder was surprisingly long. When Grace reached the bottom, she was perturbed to find a tuft of frizzy white hair and a name badge saying *Margaret Taylor-Smythe – Gatekeeping Troll Manager*.

Mr Harris burped loudly.

Grace whispered to Kenny to look away as she helped Frank jump down from the ladder, then kicked the badge out of sight. Max and Eamon followed. Quietly, they took in their surroundings.

The dusty, cobbled street, the strange wonky buildings of all shapes and sizes, the foreboding, thundery-looking sky. Grace's memories of her first visit, a few weeks before, came flooding back. There seemed to be an unusual chill to the air. Strange noises carried through it – howling, tapping, breathy laughter and, oddly, some distant classical music.

'Good grief,' said Max. 'I remember this. Is that classical music I can hear?'

'That'll be a yeti,' said Mr Harris dismissively. 'They love classical music. Anyway, come on! If we have to be in this wretched place, let's make it quick.' He stomped off down the road.

Grace, Kenny, Frank, Eamon and Max hurried after him, dodging a raucous gang of

Parent Punishers, all wearing crooked ties, some carrying whoopee cushions and stink bombs. A Pant Parader sprinted past them, a pair of pants on her head, two frizzy red bunches poking through the leg holes. She wore another pair over her trousers, like a peculiar superhero. A Roof Ruiner chucked a crumbly tile at them from behind a chimney on the roof of a grocery store. Mr Harris caught it in his mouth, like a pro, and announced delightedly that it was gingerbread.

Very soon, the shops and buildings began to look familiar.

'Burger Thing,' whispered Frank.

'Oh! The bakery!' said Grace. 'It's terrible.'

Mr Harris gave a thumbs-down. 'It's gone downhill,' he said. Then, 'Oh, what are you doing here?'

A figure was slumped in the doorway to Bitey Joe's. It had skinny legs and a big pot belly. Its four arms dangled listlessly by its side. In one hand it held an ice-cream scoop.

'Mr 'Arris?' the sad-looking figure whispered. 'You 'ave come to save Marietto? Oh, *grazie, grazie*. My 'ero!'

Mr Harris poked him. 'Are you contagious?'

'No, of courrrse not!' said Marietto. 'But my bottom! It hurrrts so much!' He shook three angry fists towards the shop door behind him.

'Marietto?' said Eamon, appearing from behind Mr Harris.

'Aaaay!' said Marietto, immediately perking up. 'It's my frrrriend Aymon! Where 'ave you been, brrrother? I 'ave missed you, and your wonderful bakerrry! Just look at it now – it is a rrruin! Brrreaks my 'eart!'

'Do you *know* each other?' Mr Harris asked in disbelief. 'This mad Gelato Guzzler is *my* undercover source of information! How do *you* know him?'

'Marietto was a regular when we had Cookie Monsters,' Eamon explained. 'He was the only one who knew we were here accidentally and that we weren't actually monsters.'

'You can tell from de nose and de eyes!' announced Marietto, pointing to his own eyes and nose with three of his hands.

'I'm so sorry, Marietto. This place would be a perfect ice-cream parlour,' said Eamon.

'It is not yourrr fault, my frrriend,' said

Marietto. He turned towards Bitey Joe's and hissed, 'It is *'is* fault. The bitey maniac. And now it 'as gone one step further – 'e bit my plumptious bottom! De pain! De itch! It is unbearrrable!' Marietto threw two hands against his forehead. 'I only came to trrry and rrreason with 'im about dis place! My *belissima gelateria*.'

'Marietto, is Bitey Joe inside? I mean, right now?' asked Grace urgently.

The Gelato Guzzler nodded miserably and pointed limply to the door.

'Fine. Let's get this over and done with,' said Mr Harris. He scooped up Marietto, propped him against a snoozing Drain Dribbler who sat against the wall, and pushed the door until it sprang open.

CHAPTER FIFTEEN

Doughnuts!

The smell hit them the moment they entered. Piles of mouldy fruit and vegetables festered in every corner and the once neat, orderly glass cabinets were filled with every kind of food imaginable. A jar of strawberry jam nestled by a packet of ham that had turned blue and furry, while a boiled egg perched precariously on top of a profiterole mountain. There were pointy bite marks in almost everything for sale and many of the items were branded with the logos of well-known human supermarkets.

Eamon shook his head sadly. 'Lou would hate

this. She made it so pretty, even if she did have to decorate her cakes with millipedes and beetle droppings.'

Frank heaved. 'Oh my goblins, it stinks!'

Kenny had thrown himself across Grace's nostrils in a heroic bid to stop the smell finding its way in. He had stretched his arms so they were long enough for him to hold on to one of her ears, while his toes clung on to her other ear, crab-like. He looked like a very long, skinny, badly placed moustache.

Grace gently prised him off. 'Thank you, Kenny, but I'm scared you'll fall off. Maybe go into my pocket, then you could pack your nose with fluff.'

Reluctantly the little Key Catcher agreed, tucked his knees into his chest and bombed into Grace's pocket.

'Right, Max, Dad, shall we split up and search for him?' Grace whispered.

They nodded but Max seemed

worried. 'I think we're going to have to. We're not very prepared, though. What did the Monster Scanner say was best to destroy him with?'

'A garlic and herb savoury muffin, with plenty of baking powder,' said Grace.

'Applied directly to the f-fangs,' murmured Frank.

'I'll just eat him,' Mr Harris said. 'It will be much quicker. I don't recall having eaten a Bottom Biter before. I hope they don't taste of bottoms.'

'No!' Grace exclaimed. 'This monster causes a horrible rash – goodness knows what could happen if you ate him. Plus, he's human-sized.'

'You know that isn't a problem, Doughnut Lady. I've eaten everyone in your family except Max and your sister. Shrimp Boy doesn't count as he's so small, but your mum and dad went in at the same time! I can manage one skinny Bottom Biter, poisonous or otherwise,' Mr Harris said self-importantly.

Grace gave him a look, then turned to Max and her dad. 'I haven't got a garlic and herb savoury muffin but I have got a blueberry one in my bag, plus loads of baking powder. It's worth a try.'

'Okay, but at any sign of danger, we meet back here. If anything goes wrong, we'll use a code word to warn each other,' Max said.

Grace nodded. 'Doughnuts.'

Mr Harris whipped round. 'Where? Yum!' His face fell as he remembered that 'doughnuts' was the code word, not a tasty treat. 'Let's get this over and done with. Doughnut Lady comes with me. Shrimp Boy clings to you, Max and Doughnut Lady's dad. See you when I've eaten this toothy madman.'

The further into the building they got, the darker it became. Black material had been hung over every window to stop any light coming in. Eamon, Max and Frank went to check out the back of the shop, while Grace and Mr Harris ventured up the creaky, twisty staircase.

'Shhh!' said Grace. 'You're so clunky and loud.'

The cyclops stopped and turned to her. 'You're bossy and annoying.'

'I'm not going to argue,' she said. 'And will you please take this?' She held out a tub of baking powder.

'I have *this*,' said Mr Harris, jabbing a finger towards his mouth. 'I'm not touching that dynamite, thank you very much.'

There was a landing at the top of the stairs, with three doors off it. All were closed. Mr Harris strode over to the one on the left and pushed it open.

'Bathroom,' he said, sounding bored. 'Nothing to report in here except awful choice of tiles. Your parents probably put them up when they lived here.'

Grace ignored him and quietly pushed open the middle door. A neatly made bed was the main feature of the room. The way the sheet was turned over made her think of the way her mum made the beds at the bakery, and she wondered if anyone had slept in it since her parents had left.

The last door was locked so Grace sent Kenny into the keyhole. Within seconds, they were in. Inside was another untouched bed, but this room was slightly different. It had black curtains up at the windows. One curtain had partly fallen off the pole it hung from. Daylight streamed into half of the room. A sturdy wooden beam stretched across the whole ceiling, with several bats dangling from it, snoozing. Mr Harris slid a bat along the beam and looked underneath at the wood. He sniffed intently.

'Urgh. Bats' feet stink, but I can also smell the bitey bottom idiot. He's been up here, hanging from his own cheesy trotters,' he said, an expression of disgust on his face.

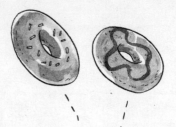

Grace looked up, then towards a wardrobe in the corner of the room. 'We need to check in there,' she mouthed. Kenny held his finger up to his lips in a bid to encourage Mr Harris to move quietly. But, rather than tiptoeing up to the cupboard, Mr Harris marched over and wrenched the door open.

A huge crash and a muffled shout of 'DOUGHNUTS!' made Grace jump violently. But the noise hadn't come from anywhere near the wardrobe; it had come from downstairs.

'Quick!' she yelled. Kenny swung from her hair like a monkey, ready to leap into action.

'Ooh, doughnuts!' cried Mr Harris in delight, elbowing her out of the way.

They hurtled down the stairs, just in time to see Max, in the darkness, carrying Frank over one shoulder in a fireman's lift, towards the front of the shop. Eamon was behind him, a pot of baking powder held above his head, ready to be launched.

It took Grace's eyes a few seconds to adjust to the light when they all reached the front of the higgledy-piggledy building.

'Where are the doughnuts?' said Mr Harris, whipping his head round, his eye scanning every millimetre of space.

Grace stared at him, waiting for him to remember.

'Oh, stupid code word. Again. Tricking me,' he said through gritted teeth.

Grace turned to Max, Eamon and Frank. 'What happened?'

Max looked anxious. Beads of sweat had formed on his forehead. 'He attacked us,' he said. 'Came flying out of a cupboard before we had time to do anything. Frank's been bitten!'

'Frank! Are you okay?' exclaimed Grace.

He nodded. 'D-Dad, you can p-put me down now.'

Max lowered him gently to the ground. Frank winced as his legs took his weight.

'Is it painful?' Grace asked, her face full of concern.

Frank nodded. 'And itchy.'

Kenny leapt from Grace's shoulder onto Frank's and gently patted the side of his head. He pointed at Frank then flexed a wiry bicep.

'He is brave, Kenny, you're right,' said Grace.

Mr Harris rolled his eye. 'You'll be insisting on a group hug next.'

'We need to go,' said Max, glancing back at the door they had burst through.

'And then we need to come back,' added Eamon.

Grace nodded. 'But next time, we'll come prepared.'

CHAPTER SIXTEEN

Monsters, Monsters Everywhere (but No Bottom Biters)

Very early the following morning, Grace, Kenny, Mr Harris, Eamon and Max entered the bakery as quietly as possible. The sun was just beginning to rise, casting a warm glow over the silent streets. They had spent the night in the area around the Natural History Museum, hoping Bitey Joe might appear. It seemed sensible to confront him when he was out of his comfort zone of Monster World. Frank had gone back to the bakery to watch Danni and Louisa perfect their garlic and herb muffins; his bottom was so itchy, he was struggling to concentrate on anything else but that.

'Same again later on, then,' said Max, heading

for the living room, which was through a door marked *Private* at the back of the bakery. He and Frank were staying at the bakery while the search was ongoing, to save making middle-of-the-night journeys back and forth to the House by the River.

'Oh my goodness!' Max gasped as he pushed open the door. 'Frank! What are you doing?'

Grace peered round Max. Frank was hanging by his feet from the light in the middle of the room, scratching his bottom with his fork. 'Hey, Dad!' he said, waving. 'Hi, everyone!'

Max looked perplexed. 'Why aren't you asleep? How did you get up there?'

'I wasn't really tired!' Frank said chirpily. 'And I'm not actually sure how I got up here; I just sort of jumped and landed like this. And now I'm up here, I quite like it.'

'You're as bad as that batty Bottom Biter,' muttered Mr Harris, who was frowning at Frank from just inside the door.

'Was there any sign of him near the museum tonight?' Frank asked.

Grace shook her head. 'No. Lots of other monsters, though – there were loads of Impatience Boosters in all the queues, quite a few Pickpocket Pixies helping themselves to people's things . . . we even saw a gang of Baby Prodders. But no Bitey Joe.'

Kenny pointed his thumbs towards the floor.

With an air of disappointment, Eamon said, 'Right – time for bed. It won't be long before we're doing this all over –' He was interrupted by a shrill ring from his pocket. Frowning, he pulled his video phone from his pocket. 'Oh, it's Colonel Hardy.' He pressed the button to connect and held the phone up so everyone could see it.

Colonel Hardy's face appeared on the screen. She looked fresh and business-like, even though it was before five o'clock in the morning. 'Oh, you're all there. At four forty-seven in the morning,' she said, raising her eyebrows. 'Frank, are you upside down?'

Frank nodded and waved cheerily.

'Well, that's interesting. Now, I'm sorry to disturb you so early, but there's been a bit of an incident,' she said. 'Around eleven p.m. last night, Norman Attwood went missing.'

Mr Harris sniggered.

Colonel Hardy rolled her eyes and continued. 'He's been found. But it's where he was and what he was doing that's the concern.'

Grace leaned forward.

'Mr Attwood was found in a twenty-four-hour supermarket, behind the butcher's counter,' said Colonel Hardy, closing her eyes briefly. 'He leapt over the top and started eating a fillet of beef. Raw.'

'Norman is disgusting,' commented Mr Harris. 'And that must be against the law. Do you need me to arrest him?'

'No, Mr Harris, I do not,' the Colonel snapped. 'The point here is not so much *what* he did but *why* he did it. We have had other, similar reports of strange behaviour by victims of the Bottom Biter. They're showing vampire-like traits! It's absolutely vital that we find this monster as quickly as possible, and work out how to cure the victims' rash – and, hopefully, their very peculiar actions.'

Grace turned slowly from the video phone and looked at Frank. He stared back at her, his eyes wide. Kenny covered his mouth with his hand.

'Am I t-t-turning into a B-Bottom Biter?' Frank said, dropping from the light fitting and landing smoothly on his feet.

Grace noticed how naturally he had swooped down. She shook her head, determined to reassure him. 'No, it's just a side effect. I'm sure it'll stop as soon as the rash goes.'

'Shrimp Boy! A Bottom Biter! Well, this is an excellent twist.' Mr Harris chortled. 'You can be Shrimp Bat from now on!'

From the screen, Colonel Hardy scowled at Mr Harris. 'Find the monster,' she said. 'We are lucky Norman Attwood wasn't recognised. It could have made the headlines.'

'We'll double our efforts, Colonel,' said Max.

Colonel Hardy gave a curt nod and cut the call.

'Well, good luck with that,' said Mr Harris. 'I can't help. As you know, I've got my days off now.'

'You're not going to come later?' asked Grace.

'Absolutely not!' said Mr Harris. 'I have completed my working hours.'

'So have we, but we're still going. This is important, Mr Harris!' said Grace.

Mr Harris shrugged. 'Take Shrimp Bat – he is now a terrifying creature of the night. He'll know what to do.' He chuckled.

'Mr Harris, please!' Grace pleaded. 'We're a team.'

'No, thank you,' said Mr Harris. 'And anyway, I will be going on my postponed trip, so I can't come with you.'

'Where are you going?' asked Grace.

'Nosy Doughnut Lady,' snapped Mr Harris. 'It's a private trip and you're not invited. I will be leaving shortly.'

'You're going now?' interjected Max. 'Shouldn't you get some sleep first, Mr Harris? You've had a long night.'

'Yes, I have, thanks to all of you,' grumbled Mr Harris. 'And, no, sleep is for weaklings. I'll snooze later when I have reached my secret destination.'

With that, he stomped up the stairs to get his bags.

'Fine,' said Grace as the door shut behind him. 'He can go on his trip. And we can check the Monster Scanner in the morning to find out where he is. It won't be a secret then, will it, Mr Harris?'

CHAPTER SEVENTEEN

The Suspicious Hand

When Grace opened her eyes the next morning, her first thought was of the Monster Scanner and Mr Harris's whereabouts. She rushed downstairs in her pyjamas, found Frank, who was drawing at the bakery counter (with sunglasses on), then bolted up to the attic.

The Monster Scanner was switched on but had a blank screen. It had timed out. Kenny was sitting cross-legged by the keyboard, twisting a paper clip into the shape of a key. He waved cheerily at her.

Grace jiggled the mouse and the screen

immediately lit up, displaying an empty search box. She frowned, fleetingly wondered why it wasn't showing the home page as it usually did, and typed in:

Mr Harris, Cyclops

His profile flashed up, showing all the information Grace already knew. She scanned through his strengths, weaknesses, likes (a new one had been added – baking) and dislikes, until she reached the bottom of the screen. Location.

'Are you trying to find out where Mr Harris has gone?' Frank asked, appearing silently in the doorway.

'Yes, I am,' said Grace chirpily. 'Here! Oh . . . Bournemouth International Conference Centre? Why would he be there?'

Frank combed his blond curls with his fork. 'Click on it. Check out their website and we can see if anything is happening there,' he suggested.

Grace clicked the mouse and waited, impatiently drumming her fingers on the desk. 'This weekend, we are proud to host the Association of Maths Teachers' Annual Conference,' she read aloud. 'Why on earth is Mr Harris at a maths teachers' conference?'

'Does he like maths?' asked Frank.

'It's not listed as a like on his profile,' said Grace.

'Perhaps he's just staying nearby?' suggested Frank.

'But what's in Bournemouth?' said Grace. 'I have a funny feeling about this.'

Frank nodded. 'I know what you mean. Perhaps he knows someone there?'

Suddenly, Kenny bounced into Grace's line of sight. He was pointing to Mr Harris's room and then to the Monster Scanner.

'Do you think he's been using it?' Grace said to the Key Catcher. Kenny nodded vigorously then used both hands to

135

roll the mouse wheel down to the search history option.

'Good idea, Kenny!' said Grace, clicking on it. 'Let's see what he's been looking up. That might give us a clue.'

No searches listed

'The search history has been cleared,' said Grace. 'That's strange. We never clear the search history, so we can check back on monsters if we need to.'

'Mr Harris must have done it,' agreed Frank.

'What's he searching for?' said Grace. 'And why does he need to hide it? It's very suspicious . . . And speaking of suspicious, while we're up here, shall we watch the CCTV footage from when the TV judge went missing? Mr Harris was very keen not to discuss that case.'

Grace got up and Frank took her place at the computer. 'I downloaded it yesterday,' Frank said, typing in a link and clicking on it.

The footage showed the private interior of the London Palladium where *Britain's Got Talent* was filmed. On the day he went missing, the head judge, a dark-haired man wearing a white T-shirt and jeans, could be seen walking down a corridor and opening a door with a shiny, silver plaque that said *Dressing Room 1*. As the judge walked into the room he jumped, as though he had been surprised by something, then he disappeared very quickly inside.

Grace frowned. 'Can you rewind that, Frank, and play it again but really slowly?'

Frank moved the footage back and slowed it down.

Grace watched the judge open the door again. He looked relaxed, his phone in his left hand, his right hand pushing the door. Then he looked up and jumped back in surprise. This time, with the video playing more slowly, she caught sight of something else. Something that most people would have missed. Another hand. A slightly green hand. And the cuff of a scruffy tweed jacket. Even in slow motion, the movement was quick as a flash. The hand grabbed the TV judge by the shoulder and pulled him into the room.

'Did someone grab him?' asked Frank nervously. He rewound the video a few seconds, zoomed in on the door and the judge, and played it again.

'Not just someone,' Grace said, closing her eyes and taking a deep breath. 'It was Mr Harris.'

CHAPTER EIGHTEEN

Mr Harris Confesses

When Mr Harris arrived back at the bakery three days later, Grace and Frank were in the study, mapping out the most recent Bottom Biter attacks. Grace heard the cyclops try to sneak past and into his own room, and cleared her throat loudly. 'Welcome back,' she called.

Mr Harris peered round the door. 'Many thanks, Doughnut Lady,' he said, then glanced at Frank and nodded. 'Shrimp Bat.' He did a double take. 'Are you eating raw bacon?'

Frank nodded. 'It's the rash. Can't stop. Sorry.'

From the desk, Kenny waved enthusiastically.

Mr Harris stared at him for a few seconds then looked away, muttering under his breath.

'So, where did you go?' Grace asked. 'Did you have a nice time while we were here, working every night, dealing with more attacks? You'll be interested to know that the victims are behaving more bizarrely by the minute. One has even grown fangs!'

The cyclops turned to her. 'I went somewhere and it was satisfactory,' he replied. Then he darted into his room and shut the door.

Grace spoke loudly. 'Did you get a nice whiff of sea air?' she called out. 'Do any multiplication?'

Everything remained silent and still for what seemed like an age. Frank clutched his fork tighter and Kenny hid behind the Monster Scanner's keyboard. Slowly, the door to Mr Harris's room creaked open. 'Have you been *spying* on me?' he asked, his eye peering through the gap.

'No. We've barely left the bakery, have we, Frank?' replied Grace.

Frank shook his head.

'Yes, you have!' exclaimed the cyclops, throwing the door open, outraged. 'I knew it! I knew you couldn't stop being a pest. And NOSY! And needing to know EVERYTHING! So, go on then, Doughnut Lady, give me your lecture on how going away to the seaside to eat an ice cream and a couple of people is *unacceptable*. I'm ready!' He folded his arms dramatically and stared hard at Grace.

'Eat a couple of people?' said Grace.

Mr Harris looked shocked, then flustered.

'Er . . . no,' he ventured.

'Is that why you went away?' asked Grace smoothly. 'I thought the Prime Minister, and Dad, and Max *and* I had all said you can't work for the Secret Service and eat people!'

'Oh my goblins,' whispered Frank.

Kenny lay flat and silently rolled under the keyboard until he was completely out of view.

'Oh, Doughnut Lady, don't make a fuss. It's no big deal,' the cyclops said huffily.

Grace shook her head in disbelief. 'They're people, Mr Harris! You can't just eat them!'

'But I'm so good now,' he whined. 'I am so much pickier. I only eat people who I am absolutely certain won't be missed by anyone!'

'You went to a conference for maths teachers!' cried Grace.

'Exactly,' hissed Mr Harris.

'Mr Harris! This is terrible! How many did you eat?' Grace demanded.

'Only two,' he snapped. 'They were old and sooo boring, but one was surprisingly tasty. Undertones of Ovaltine and just a hint of digestive biscuit.' He licked his lips and rubbed his tummy absentmindedly.

'Did they taste meaty too?' Frank blurted out. He immediately clamped his hand over his mouth in horror.

'Shrimp Bat, a little control, please,' barked Mr Harris.

'I'm trying to fight the urges,' said Frank plaintively. 'But it's so hard! You saw me with the raw bacon . . .'

Mr Harris threw his head back and laughed raucously. 'Oh, Shrimp Bat,' he said, breathless. 'You crack me up. Finally, a Hunter I can get on board with!'

Grace stared at the cyclops. 'It's not funny.

And, actually, while we're on the subject of eating people, is there anything you want to tell us about the case you've been given? The head judge for *Britain's Got Talent* who is missing?'

Mr Harris's face remained impassive. 'No.'

'Nothing?'

He shook his huge head and studied one of his yellowing fingernails.

'Did you go to his dressing room at the London Palladium and eat him?' asked Grace quietly.

'No, that absolutely wasn't me or something I did,' said Mr Harris.

'Mr Harris,' said Grace, 'it sounds very much like something you *would* do. And, if you did, you need to tell me so that we can work out how on earth to deal with the situation.'

'Not me. Nope,' the cyclops confirmed.

'There's e-evidence,' said Frank.

Mr Harris whipped his head round, checking if anyone else was listening. He shrugged. 'Fine – I might have had a moment of

weakness and treated myself to
something gourmet after we destroyed
my grandfather,' he gabbled. 'But there is
definitely no evidence, so it's fine. The only
evidence went in here.' He pointed towards
his enormous mouth. 'But sssh.' He held a finger
up to his lips. 'We will tell the Prime Minister
he's safe and well and living in Texas, USA,' he
added, clearly delighted at his brilliant idea.

Grace raised her eyebrows. 'And what will we
tell them when they ask us what we found on the
CCTV?'

A look of shock passed over the cyclops's face.
Kenny popped out from under the keyboard and
pressed 'play'. Mr Harris watched the footage in
silence, asking for it to be rewound and replayed
eleven times.

'That elegant hand could be anybody's,' he
said eventually.

'Mr Harris,' said Grace firmly, 'we need to
come up with a plan to deal with this situation.

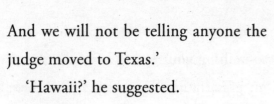

And we will not be telling anyone the judge moved to Texas.'

'Hawaii?' he suggested.

'Nowhere!' snapped Grace. 'We will have to tell the truth eventually, but it's possible we can buy some time before we have to do that . . . if we catch Bitey Joe.'

The cyclops frowned.

'But we need you here, helping us. No clocking off before the job is done or sneaking off to eat teachers,' she said. 'You need to be part of the team.'

Mr Harris sighed heavily. 'You will be my downfall, Doughnut Lady. Fine. But you have to promise that I won't get in trouble for eating the judge. It was a lapse in judgement. And he tasted expensive and delicious. But it won't happen again.'

'I'll do what I can, but I can't promise

that you won't be in trouble. You ate a really well-known TV star, after all,' she replied.

'For goodness' sake,' muttered Mr Harris. 'It's not like it was Ant or Dec!'

CHAPTER NINETEEN

The Cake Shack

Just a few hours later, Grace, Kenny, Max, Eamon and Mr Harris found themselves back in South Kensington.

'You look ridiculous,' Mr Harris said to Frank, who was wearing oven mitts and a gum shield. His fork poked out of the pocket of his jeans as he was unable to hold it with the mitts on.

Frank looked downcast. 'Sorry. I know,' he spluttered. 'It's hard to speak with this gum shield but I have to wear it – I just don't trust myself at the moment. And the mitts stop me scratching.'

They were standing outside a temporary food

shack, not far from the entrance to the Natural History Museum.

'What is this?' demanded Mr Harris.

'While you were off on your *trip*,' Grace said pointedly, 'we came up with a plan. This is the Cake Shack, a pop-up bakery, and we are going to use it to lure Bitey Joe to lots of irresistible human food he will definitely want to come and steal.'

'That's a terrible plan,' said the cyclops. 'But I love cakes, so it's not all bad.'

The shack was painted yellow like Cake Hunters, raised off the ground on a platform, and had an illuminated giant iced doughnut and chocolate muffin perched on its roof. Even before they had displayed any of the delicious treats they had brought from the bakery, the Cake Shack was getting people's attention.

While Grace and Eamon arranged doughnuts and cakes on stands, Kenny sat on the roof of the shack, keeping a lookout for anything suspicious.

Max, Frank and Mr Harris wandered towards the museum, giving out flyers advertising the pop up bakery. Mr Harris wasn't taking no for an answer. If anyone he approached didn't take a flyer, he stuffed one into the hood of their jacket, or into the top of their rucksack, or on top of their baby's pram. He was so big, no one argued with him.

Grace seemed to be the only one who had noticed that, every now and again, Frank would swoop forward, his arms spread out, a bit like bat wings. She was worried about him, and more determined than ever to find the troublesome Bottom Biter – and a cure for the people he had nibbled.

Grace watched them handing out flyers as she laid doughnuts on a tray. Mr Harris walked up the steps to the Natural History Museum and disappeared inside, clutching a bunch of flyers.

'He's going to drop a few flyers round near the dinosaurs,' said Max, arriving back at the shack with Frank. 'I said to sneak some into the top of the trapdoor if he gets the chance.

Monsters are so nosy, they should get picked up and taken to Monster World in no time.'

Frank glanced at a digital device on his left wrist. It was linked to the Monster Scanner back at the House by the River.

'It's showing 247 monsters within a 100-metre radius,' he said, recoiling as he caught a waft of garlic, rising from some muffins Grace had kept behind the counter.

'That's a lot for a very small area,' said Eamon from inside the shack. 'There's clearly more activity around the gateway.'

Max raised a finger to his lips and jerked his head towards a very tall, thin man, wearing a long raincoat and a pair of sunglasses, who was approaching the counter.

'First customer,' Max said.

The man walked very slowly, wobbling from left to right. When he reached the counter, he pointed to the stack of white chocolate and raspberry doughnuts and held up six fingers.

Large, rather fuzzy fingers. Eamon, who was delighted to have a customer, didn't seem to notice his peculiar-looking hands. He bustled around putting doughnuts into boxes.

'Dad?' said Grace quietly. 'I'm not sure this customer is –'

'I'm back,' interrupted Mr Harris, appearing at the counter, leaning towards the displays and inhaling deeply. 'I threw at least one hundred flyers down the Monster World ladder.' He stopped speaking and did a double take at the tall, thin customer. Grace saw him glance at the fuzzy hands. With no warning, he whipped open the man's raincoat.

'Mr Harris!' cried Eamon. 'Oh!'

Under the raincoat was a tower of six Snack Snafflers, each standing on another's shoulders. The one at the top held a pair of sunglasses while balancing unsteadily on the shoulders of the next one, who was holding the raincoat round himself and his friends. The next one down had his arms

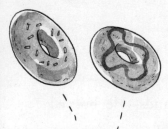

through the raincoat's sleeves and was the owner of the large fuzzy hands.

'I knew it. Snack Snafflers. Shoo!' bellowed Mr Harris. 'I know you won't have any money to pay for our top-quality goods! Go away!'

The Snack Snafflers began to jump off each other's shoulders and hurry off towards the museum, blending into the crowds. But before one of them could make its escape, Mr Harris picked it up by its stubby tail and strode round to the back of the Cake Shack.

'H-He's going to eat it!' said Frank, pointing with his fork.

Grace leapt down the steps from the shack and found Mr Harris holding up the Snack Snaffler, who was trying to kick him from mid-air.

'Stop it,' said Mr Harris, using his free hand to take a bunch of flyers out of his pocket. He stuffed them into the creature's hands. 'Now listen to me. Take these to Monster World and post them through the letterbox at Bitey Joe's.'

The Snack Snaffler hissed and shook its head.

'Fine,' said Mr Harris. 'Then before I eat you, hand over those sunglasses.' He dangled the monster over his giant mouth. It wriggled and writhed, and swung and twisted, until eventually it went still and scowled. It threw its sunglasses to the ground.

'Well done. Now, are you going to post the flyers at Bitey Joe's?' demanded Mr Harris.

The Snack Snaffler nodded grumpily.

'Very good,' said the cyclops. 'I have spies, so I will know if you don't do it, and I will eat you. Clear?'

The creature gave one curt nod and narrowed its mean, dark eyes.

'Lovely,' said Mr Harris, shaping the monster into a ball and lobbing him overarm towards the Natural History Museum. The Snack Snaffler tore through the air like lightning, gently skimming the heads of passers-by, before disappearing neatly into the entrance of the building.

'Excellent shot. You've still got it, Secret Agent Harris.' The cyclops said to himself, giggling. 'Oh, Doughnut Lady, you're creepily watching me without me knowing.'

Grace found herself giggling with him. 'That was an excellent shot,' she said. 'Well done for not eating the Snaffler.'

Mr Harris waved a hand dismissively. 'You never know where a Snack Snaffler has been with those grabby hands. And they have a rather stodgy, sticky texture that plays havoc with my palate.'

'Obviously,' said Grace, nodding.

'Now,' said Mr Harris, plonking himself down on the ground and popping on the discarded sunglasses 'because of my unbelievable quick thinking, my extraordinary source-handling and heroic actions, that daft Bottom Biter will be here in no time, so fetch me three no-bang muffins and then I'll have a power nap.'

CHAPTER TWENTY

Bitey Joe's Great Escape

Mr Harris's power nap lasted almost two hours. While he snored behind the Cake Shack, the Hunters were run off their feet, selling cake after cake after cake. They had been visited by several monsters who had picked up flyers in Monster World. Like the Snack Snafflers in the raincoat, some had gone to the effort of disguising themselves (badly) as humans, and even paid with proper money. Unfortunately, a couple of them didn't do quite so well. A Coin Clincher and a Handbag Hider, both known for their liking of other people's things, had sneaked

into the back of the shack and stolen a couple of the special, monster-destroying cakes which had been stashed safely underneath the counter, out of view.

The Coin Clincher exploded almost straight away. Eamon had to shield some doughnuts from the gold and silver fireworks, while human customers oohed and aahed at what they thought was a spectacular effort by the shack staff to attract more cake-buyers. The Handbag Hider blew up almost on top of Mr Harris as it fled the pop-up bakery. Despite the deafening crack it made as it disintegrated into a ball of sparkly pink dust, Mr Harris slept on, like a very large, ugly baby. Unfortunately, he also snored contentedly as a cloaked figure crept up the wooden steps at the back of the shack. The figure's long, sharp nose sniffed intently, and two pointy fangs protruded over thin, pale lips.

Grace and Eamon were busy serving an endless line of customers who couldn't get enough of the Cake Shack's inventive flavours of muffins and doughnuts – salted caramel and banana, chocolate and chilli, strawberry and elderflower, lime and coconut – so they didn't see the tall, slim, toothy figure glide in soundlessly behind them.

Just as Grace bent down to get more supplies from under the counter to refill the stands, her eyes straining to see the labels in the low light, a smooth, slender hand shot out in front of her and snatched one of the boxes. Grace yelped in surprise and automatically reached for a pot of baking powder, flicking the lid off with her thumb. As she threw it into the air, the Bottom Biter reached up and caught it, spilling none at all, and hissed menacingly at her. With the hiss came a waft of mint. Grace saw a length of floss caught between his left fang and the tooth beside it. His monster profile really had been very accurate on the dental hygiene front.

'Mr Harris!' she screeched. 'WAKE UP! NOW!'

'Hush, Doughnut Lady,' came a mumble from outside. 'You'll wake me up from my power nap . . .'

'Bitey Joe is HERE!' she bellowed. Eamon seized another pot of baking powder and took off the lid.

'No,' came another mutter. 'No sign of him yet . . . now, for goodness' sake, shhh. I'm snoozing.'

'HE'S HERE!' Grace shouted at the top of her voice.

There was a rustle and a clank from outside.

'Where?' came a snappy, confused response.

Eamon lobbed another pot of baking powder past Grace and towards Bitey Joe, but the Bottom Biter dodged it skilfully, flying through the air and out of the door. As he leapt, three wrapped toffees and a Chomp sailed out of a pocket

inside the folds of his cloak. At the same time, Mr Harris heaved himself to his feet. Bitey Joe flew straight into his back and his box of stolen muffins spilled all over the ground.

'Wasteful!' cried Mr Harris, bending over to pick up the cakes. 'Ow, OW, OUCH!'

With terrifying speed, Bitey Joe had sunk his fangs into the cyclops's bottom.

Mr Harris straightened up in a millisecond. As his mouth formed another 'Ow', the brazen Bottom Biter threw the tub of baking powder he had caught directly into the cyclops's mouth. With a venomous hiss he was gone.

Then Mr Harris exploded.

CHAPTER TWENTY-ONE

The Pursuit

'We need to go, Dad!' said Grace.

Cries came from the queue of customers who were waiting to be served.

'Yes, of course!' Eamon replied, pushing all the muffins and doughnuts that were left to the front of the hatch. 'Free cakes for everyone! Please don't all dash at once – take it in turns! And if you like the cakes, come and visit us at Cake Hunters in Camden . . .' He snapped the shutters closed and hurried out of the shack just behind Grace. As they slammed the door, Kenny leapt off the roof and landed neatly in Grace's pocket.

Frank
and Max
were waiting for
them at the front of the
yellow pop-up bakery, where
all the customers were distracted
by the free cakes in front of them.

'Mr Harris has exploded!' said Grace. 'Bitey Joe threw baking powder straight into his mouth.'

'I wondered what that almighty crash was,' said Max.

'We need to get to Monster World,' said Frank. 'Bitey Joe ran off towards the museum. I saw him!'

They ran towards the entrance. Just inside, they found two members of staff upset and wincing in pain while scratching their bottoms.

'Sorry, you can't go in,' said one. 'There's been an incident with a man in fancy dress . . . we're about to call the police.'

'No need,' said Max, holding up an identity card. 'We work for the government and we'll deal with the incident.'

Eamon nodded. 'Please shut the door, don't let anyone else in, and don't discuss what has happened here with anyone until we're back.'

They rushed out of the foyer towards the dinosaur exhibition, then darted behind the T-Rex backdrop. Max lifted the trapdoor and revealed the rickety ladder. The top rung had changed from the last time they had visited – it was now a flute.

Grace started to descend the ladder.

'Grace!' called Frank. 'What if there's a troll at the bottom?'

She paused, rummaged in the pocket of her jeans and held up a tub of powder. 'Don't worry, I've got this!'

She carried on descending, treading on all sorts of strange and improvised ladder rungs – a javelin, a Rapunzel-like blonde plait, a long bone, and what Grace was sure looked like – and smelled like – a dead, dried-up eel. As she neared the bottom of the ladder, the bright, full Monster World moon cast more than enough light for her to make out the top of a head covered in thick black hair.

Quietly, she eased the lid off the tub of baking powder and shook some out over the troll. She braced herself for the bang and hoped it wouldn't be too fireworky, given that she was directly above.

She waited. And waited.

But nothing happened.

She glanced down and saw that the troll was in exactly the same place, but now it had a scattering of fine white powder glinting on its head.

She sprinkled some more. The troll glanced at its shoulder and brushed off the powder that had landed there. But it still didn't explode.

Grace tipped the tub upside down and shook it until it was empty.

The troll looked up. It was male. It had a
rather human face, but its teeth were so big and
white, and its skin so orange, it was unlikely to
be a person.

'Who are you?' he asked. Grace thought she
could detect a hint of nervousness in his voice.

'We're here on official business,' she said, trying to sound grown-up and authoritative.

'Oh,' stammered the orange troll. 'Fine. Come through, then.' He got to his feet – he was tall for a troll – and moved out of the way. Grace had expected at least twenty more questions, an argument and possibly some sort of fight, so the fact that he had given up and let them through so easily confused her.

'Oh, thank you,' she said, jumping down from the ladder, followed by her dad and Max. Frank swooped gracefully down from ten rungs above them. It was quite a change to the last time he had descended, quivering with nerves.

'Pleasure,' the troll replied, winking.

Grace noticed that he seemed rather good-natured for a troll and that he also, for some reason, looked vaguely familiar. She wondered if she might have seen him on a previous visit to Monster World, but quickly pushed the thought out of her mind when she saw the back of a scruffy tweed jacket she recognised not far ahead.

'Mr Harris!' she called.

The cyclops turned round, a murderous look on his face, his eye bulging. 'That toothy buffoon bit my bottom!' he yelled. 'And it itches and stings and it's UNBEARABLE. Get the muffins out and explode that tyrant immediately. I must have revenge!'

'The garlic and herb muffins,' Eamon whispered as they caught up with him. 'They're still in the Cake Shack!'

Mr Harris went very still. 'You forgot to bring them?'

'I'm so sorry,' said Eamon. 'It's my fault. I'll go back and get them.'

Mr Harris took a deep breath. 'Doughnut Lady's dad, you have no idea, whatsoever, of how terrible my bottom feels. It HURTS. It ITCHES. I am INJURED. I EXPLODED. All in the LINE OF DUTY. And you? You forgot the only thing that can explode that fanged fool? Go and get me my REVENGE MUFFINS!'

'Oh, for goodness' sake, stop being dramatic,' said Grace. 'We just need to think . . .'

Suddenly a voice came from behind them. '*Buonasera*, my frrriends! It's just possible that I might be able to 'elp . . .'

CHAPTER TWENTY-TWO

Marietto Lends Some Hands

'Marietto Montabula in Grindelbug,' Mr Harris said curtly, scratching his bottom. 'Why are you here, stealing the limelight?'

'*Ciao*, my frrriend!' Marietto said happily, air-kissing both sides of the cyclops's face. 'I 'ave come to 'elp. I always keep an eye on what dis monstrrrrous bat-man is doing and I 'ave seen 'im rush back into 'is disgusting shop. Then I saw you appear in de rrrroad and you are scrrratching your bottom! I think you've been bitten by the scoundrrrrel!' He shook three see-through fists at the door. The last held an empty ice-cream tub.

'It might be too dangerous to help, Marietto,' said Grace. 'You don't want to be bitten again.'

'No, I do not!' cried Marietto. 'But it is fine because I am not going inside. I couldn't 'elp but 'ear you say you 'ave forgotten de muffins to destroy bitey bat-face. It is lucky that I 'ave an alternative of my own just 'ere.' One of the

Gelato Guzzler's hands shot behind him and produced an elaborate silver tray with a domed silver lid on it. Another hand whipped the dome off, revealing a shiny ice-cream cone holder, full of waffled cornets holding perfectly swirly white ice cream, with dots of yellow and green sprinkled over it. They smelled overpoweringly of garlic. Grace noticed that, behind Max, Frank was holding his nose and appeared rather green and sickly.

'My new garrrlic and 'erb ice cream! It is *bellissimo*! And . . .' Marietto winked at them. 'I 'ave added de special ingrrredient – baking powderrr! I even bought it frrrom dis shop! 'E sold it to me, not knowing it could be 'is downfall!'

'Oh, thank you!' said Grace, as Kenny high-fived Marietto. 'But how did you know which ingredients to use to destroy him?'

'I 'eard you talking inside the shop when I was outside with my poor bitten bottom! I decided then that I would crrreate a special flavourrr gelato in case I 'ad the chance to scoop it onto 'is fangs myself! Dis place was so beautiful beforrrre he rrrruined it! It should be mine. I can make it grrrreat again!' Marietto raised all his arms into the air. The silver tray wobbled precariously.

'We'll make sure of it!' said Frank.

'This is wonderful, Marietto,' added Eamon. 'And don't worry – we'll get you your gelateria.'

Marietto slapped Eamon on the back and kissed the side of his head. '*Grazie*, my frrrriend. Good luck! Show 'im who is de boss! Oh, and I 'ave these for back up.' He reached into his pockets with two of his hands and drew out handfuls of garlic bulbs. He passed them round to everyone, except Frank, who was gagging, then put his hands together in pairs in a prayer position. 'Be safe!' he cried.

'Again, thank you, Marietto. You just might have saved the day,' said Max.

'No!' bellowed Mr Harris. 'Four Arms has *not*

saved the day. *I* will be saving the day. Saving the day is *my* job.' He turned round and strode towards Bitey Joe's.

'Not yet, Mr Harris!' called Grace. 'We need a plan!'

A muffled response came. 'I have a plan, Doughnut Lady! Ice cream. Fangs. Bang. Day saved. By me.'

'Well, you'll need the ice cream then, won't you?' replied Grace, looking at her dad, who was now holding the tray with the numerous cones balanced on top.

The cyclops appeared in the doorway. 'I assumed you would be clever enough to follow me. *With* the ice cream. I can't believe you call yourselves monster-hunters,' he mumbled as he disappeared back inside, scratching his bottom.

Grace and the others said goodbye to Marietto and hurried after Mr Harris. The smell inside was just as bad, if not

worse, than it had been the last time. Flies, some normal-looking, some bright orange, some green with pink spots, buzzed loudly from every corner. Black material had been taped up at the windows so it was gloomy. Somehow, this made the rotten stench seem more intense and foul.

'What happened to this place? I still can't believe it. It's only been a few weeks since Lou and I left,' said Eamon.

'Bitey Joe happened,' said Grace. 'Now, what's the plan? Are we splitting up?'

Max nodded. 'Makes sense. Mr Harris can stay here and guard the door in case Bitey Joe tries to escape, and I'll do the same at the back. The rest of you can check upstairs. Eamon, you know this place better than the rest of us so you'll know where the best hiding places are.'

'Guard the door?' Mr Harris said incredulously. 'How will I do that heroically? I am by far your best asset – put me in the field!'

'This is the field, Mr Harris,' said Max.

'Actually,' said Frank. 'This is the most d-d-dangerous spot because he's most likely to try and escape through the front door.'

Mr Harris pondered for a moment. 'A well-made point by Shrimp Bat. This vampire attitude suits you. Fine. I'll do it.'

They shared the cones round. Even Kenny took one, despite it being much larger than he was. He squished the plump bulb of garlic Marietto had given him into the top of the ice cream, dangled his steely arms out of Grace's pocket and held the ice cream out in front of him.

Mr Harris sniffed his cone intently and recoiled. 'This smells awful. Which is such a shame, because I *love* ice cream.'

'It's handy you don't want to eat it,' said Grace. 'Because you'd blow up again and who knows where you'd go, seeing as you're already in Monster World.'

Mr Harris scowled. 'This really is the last straw. That bitey birdbrain has put me off my food,' he hissed. 'I will bite him and eat him, and then I will hang off a beam and have a well-deserved nap.'

Grace looked concerned. 'The sooner we find him, the better. We can't have you being any more unpredictable than you already are. Let's go.'

Mr Harris blocked the front door while Max headed towards the back of the building. Grace led the way up the rickety stairs, Frank behind her and Eamon bringing up the rear. A potent smell of garlic surrounded them. She headed straight to the master bedroom, where she and Mr Harris had encountered the sleeping bats on their previous visit. The door was ajar. Slowly she pushed it further open, her eyes adjusting to the darkness inside. The curtain had been repaired and there was hardly any light at all coming in. Grace found the torch tucked into the side of her rucksack and switched it on.

'Urgh! It stinks!' said Eamon, pinching his nose. 'And there's bat poo on my bed!'

'But it's not your bed any more!' came a menacing voice from the wardrobe. Bitey Joe leapt out of the darkness and loomed in front of them. He was much taller than Grace had realised – in fact, he was probably nearly the same height as Mr Harris. His skin had a luminescent white tinge and his fangs were like glistening razors. His limbs were long and lithe – it was easy to see that he could move swiftly and powerfully. He was one of the most terrifying creatures Grace had ever seen. The only thing that made him fractionally less frightening was the half-chewed Curly Wurly poking out of the fold of his cloak.

Suddenly, an ice cream shot through the air from below. Kenny had launched it from Grace's pocket. Although it was an excellent shot, Bitey Joe ducked at the speed of light. The ice cream flew across the room and hit the far wall.

Then Frank quickly catapulted a bulb of garlic. It was followed by one from

179

Eamon. Bitey Joe was a blur as he swerved like lightning to avoid them. Grace felt the rush of air from his movement frighteningly close to her face. Suddenly, what felt like a cold piece of wire was at her throat. She dropped her ice-cream cones and garlic, automatically reaching for her neck.

'Don't struggle,' Bitey Joe said matter-of-factly behind her. 'That's super-strength dental floss round your neck – you're not going anywhere. It has more uses than just keeping these beauties pearly white.' He flashed an evil smile at the others, his fangs sparkling like marble in the darkness.

'Grace!' cried Eamon and Frank. Eamon threw another ice-cream cone. It missed Bitey Joe by a millimetre but the Bottom Biter didn't even flinch.

'Stop!' commanded Bitey Joe. 'No more missiles. If I blow up, she blows up . . . which is exactly why she's coming with me.'

CHAPTER TWENTY-THREE

Hostage

Bitey Joe put his arm over the floss that was around Grace's throat, lifted her and bolted out of the room. Without warning, he leapt from the top of the stairs and glided to the bottom. It took less than a second. Grace tried to scream but, since the monster's arm was across her windpipe, no sound came out.

He pushed her towards the front of the shop. Grace hoped Mr Harris was still there and hadn't got bored and wandered off. As they burst through the door, Grace saw Mr Harris licking a raw, mouldy-looking steak behind the grimy

shop counter. He looked up guiltily, but when he saw who Bitey Joe had in his grasp, his guilt changed to anger.

'PUT HER DOWN!' he bellowed.

'Or what?' hissed Bitey Joe.

'Or I will explode you!' said Mr Harris, holding a melting ice-cream cone above his enormous head.

Bitey Joe sneered. 'Don't you mean you'll explode us both?'

Mr Harris frowned. 'She won't explode – she's Doughnut Lady.'

'I will make sure she *does*,' breathed the Bottom Biter.

Mr Harris shrugged. 'Well, she won't mind making the sacrifice. She's a Hunter.'

The door burst open again and Frank, Max and Eamon spilled into the room.

'She's not sacrificing anything!' said Eamon.

'That's my daughter!'

'But think how quiet it would be,' mumbled Mr Harris, scratching his bottom.

'Let her go, Joseph,' said Max calmly.

Bitey Joe threw his pale head back and laughed. 'Joseph? You sound like my mother! It's never that easy. Put down your ridiculous weapons or I will make it a very sticky end for this particular Hunter.'

Max, Frank and Eamon dropped their garlic and ice creams.

Bitey Joe looked at Mr Harris. 'Now, get out of my way, you one-eyed clown.'

Mr Harris's eye narrowed. '*What* did you call me?' He hurled the ice cream towards Bitey Joe. Although the Bottom Biter ducked, he wasn't quite fast enough. Some of the pungent ice cream dripped onto his forehead, leaving a graze that crackled and sparked. Bitey Joe let out a sinister growl, which sent a shiver up Grace's spine. Her eyes darted round for something she could grab to fight him with. But there was nothing within reach except a stale-looking baguette, which she knew would be of very little help.

As she tried to think of a plan B, out of the corner of her eye Grace detected movement. Kenny had slid out of her pocket and was racing towards Frank. She glanced up to see if Bitey Joe had noticed, but his eyes were fixed on Mr Harris. Her heart pounded as Frank carefully, with the tiniest of movements, slipped an ice-cream cone from behind his back into the Key Catcher's long, wiry arms. Kenny tiptoed back towards her, his wide eyes unblinking, staring at Bitey Joe.

Grace felt a hint of a draught as Kenny launched himself into the air and landed, with a level of precision that only a Key Catcher possessed, inside her pocket. A second later, he had guided the cone safely into her right hand.

'I'm not moving until you put her down,' said

Mr Harris, filling the space in front of the doorway.

'I'll bite her,' threatened Bitey Joe.

'*I* want to bite her!' shouted Mr Harris. 'I mean bite you – no, I mean explode you. Oh, I don't know. Your germy teeth have made me mad and wild!' He lobbed another ice cream towards his pointy-toothed enemy. Quick as a flash, Bitey Joe held up his arm, which was protected by his sleeve, and sent the ice cream hurtling back towards the cyclops. Mr Harris spun round and hunched over. The ice cream hit his back, sliding down his jacket and into the back of his trousers.

'You have got to be kidding!' yelled the cyclops. 'It's COLD and my bottom is already in a terrible state. I swear I will . . .' He stopped. He turned round and attempted to sniff his own backside. 'Oh. Something wonderful is happening. It's soothing my rash! I don't even mind the smell any more! Ha! You stupid fool, you've only gone and cured me! Some villain you are – swoop around, take a hostage, make some threats, cure an onlooker . . .' He laughed raucously.

Grace felt Bitey Joe shake with anger. He lurched forward, taking Grace with him. But he stopped in his tracks as something shiny flew towards him, bashing him on the forehead, just where the ice cream had grazed his porcelain skin. It was Frank's fork. Bitey Joe threw his head back and howled in pain and, for a split second, he loosened his grip on Grace. Without hesitation, she twisted out of his hold.

'Now, Grace!' yelled Frank.

She thrust the cone Kenny had given her up towards Bitey Joe's mouth and dropped to the floor, scurrying away from him. At the same time, the front door to the bakery burst open. Marietto staggered in, a glistening ice-cream scoop full of the special gelato in each of his hands.

'I 'ear the shouting! I 'ave to 'elp!' he cried.

As he stumbled into Mr Harris's back, a shard of bright moonlight shot through the gap in the door, swathing Bitey Joe in a milky glow.

The Bottom Biter looked up at Mr Harris and Marietto and pulled back his pale lips to reveal a row of perfectly pointy, glistening white teeth. A length of trapped dental floss wafted in the breeze between them. But as he leapt into the air, arms up and poised to attack, there was a sharp crack, then a burst of blue flames. The flames extinguished themselves in a millisecond, leaving nothing but a neat pile of black dust on the floor.

A neat pile of black dust that had once been known as Bitey Joe.

CHAPTER TWENTY-FOUR

A Gatekeeping Troll with a Difference

They left Marietto singing something loudly in Italian and sweeping up Bitey Joe's remains, pieces of ice-cream cone and garlic cloves in his newly claimed shop, which he would soon turn into the ice-cream parlour he had dreamed about.

'Shrimp Bat, have another one of these,' said Mr Harris, catching Frank by the back of his shorts and dropping a leftover ice-cream cone down them. Frank gasped as the freezing cold ice cream hit his skin, then let out a sigh.

'It's so cold but so good at the same time,' he said. 'I think you can go back to calling me

Shrimp Boy, Mr Harris. I don't feel like eating raw meat any more!'

'That's my decision, Shrimp Bat-Boy,' said the cyclops casually, 'since I just saved you all again because I threw that ice cream at Bitey Joe.' He popped some garlic down the back of his own trousers, for good measure.

'I think it was more the distraction Frank

created, Kenny's ice cream that Grace threw and the moonlight Marietto let in that might have done it,' said Max, a smile at the corner of his mouth.

'Teamwork!' said Eamon as they came up to the Human World gateway near Burger Thing. The orange troll who had been at the bottom of the ladder from the museum was there.

The troll seemed to recognise them, and said, 'Double gate duties tonight! We're short-staffed.' As his gaze travelled over the group, he saw Mr Harris and recoiled, beads of sweat forming on his brow.

Mr Harris shook his head and rolled his eye. 'It's not teamwork when I have to eat another bitter-tasting troll to get us all out of here.'

'Don't eat me again!' yelped the troll.

Mr Harris frowned and studied the troll. 'You seem familiar.'

'You ate me in my dressing room at the London Palladium,' the troll said nervously.

Grace gasped. 'I thought you looked familiar. You're alive! Thank goodness.'

Mr Harris raised his eyebrow. 'You're the judge I snacked on! When did you sneak out? I thought I had swallowed you.'

The troll-judge shook his head. 'I clung to one of your teeth so you couldn't, and you sleep very soundly, so I got out when you napped. I've been here, pretending to be a troll, ever since. I've tried to use the gateways loads of times but there's so much CCTV being installed, I'm always seen and made to come back.' There was desperation in his voice. 'Please take me back with you.'

'Of course we will,' said Grace, 'and I'm so sorry about what he did.' She shot Mr Harris a glare.

'It was one of *your* cases to solve,' said Max in disbelief.

'Eating a judge from my favourite television show was on my bucket list,' whined the cyclops. He turned to Grace and Frank. 'He can't go back. I'll be in trouble with Colonel Very Impatient!'

'What if I don't tell anyone?' blurted the troll-judge. 'If you help me leave this . . . place, I won't say a word! I'll say I got fed up of being famous and went on holiday without telling anyone!'

The cyclops paused, interested. 'To Hawaii?'

'Yes!' the troll-judge cried. 'I love Hawaii!'

Mr Harris turned to Grace. 'I told you!' he said triumphantly.

'I don't know how happy I am about this,' said Max. Eamon nodded in agreement.

'Please,' begged the troll-judge. 'Just get me out of here. No hard feelings from me.'

'And none from me,' said Mr Harris, pushing the troll-judge towards the gateway before anyone could say anything else. 'You first.'

CHAPTER TWENTY-FIVE

A Message from
the Prime Minister

Two days later, their surroundings were rather different. Grace, Kenny, Mr Harris, Frank, Max and Eamon waited outside Colonel Hardy's office. Mr Harris was reading a newspaper, the front page of which sported a smiley photo of the judge they had found in Monster World. The headline read:

BRITAIN'S GOT TALENT JUDGE

WENT ON SECRET HOLIDAY

MISSING PERSON REPORT SPARKED HUGE

MANHUNT – WHILE HE RELAXED IN HAWAII!

'You can go in now,' said a security officer standing by the office door.

Inside, Colonel Patience Hardy was leaning against her desk, waiting for them. She straightened up as they filed in. 'Welcome back,' she said, although she didn't sound very welcoming. 'Take a seat.' She gestured to two sofas around a low table, which had water, tea, coffee and biscuits laid out on it. There was also a brown envelope and a very shiny silver pen.

As Grace, Frank, Max and Eamon sat down, Mr Harris shot over to the leather chair behind the desk and plopped himself down, then wheeled over to join the others.

'Mr Harris!' whispered Grace. Colonel Hardy looked thunderous.

'May I?' the cyclops asked the Colonel.

'You already have, Mr Harris,' the Colonel snapped.

Mr Harris turned to Grace, raised his eyebrow and smiled smugly. Then he helped himself to four chocolate digestives from the tray and ate them all at once.

Colonel Hardy looked at the Hunter family and the cyclops sitting in her chair with chocolate on his chin. She took a breath. 'Prime Minister Attwood sends her apologies. As Mr Attwood –'

'You mean Norman.' Mr Harris chuckled.

Colonel Hardy glared at him. 'As Mr Attwood has recovered, now the garlic vaccine has been distributed, Mr and Mrs Attwood are attending an important engagement. However, the Prime Minister has asked me to pass on a message.' She cleared her throat and began to read from a note in her hand. '*Once again, I must thank you. What you have done has been nothing short of miraculous. You have stopped a particularly evil monster from bringing terror to the streets of London within days of being told about him. I can't tell you how grateful*

I am. I will be arranging a private lunch for you at the Houses of Parliament in due course, to show my gratitude. My husband, Norman, also sends his best wishes.'

Mr Harris stifled another giggle and enquired, 'And did *Norman* also send a note, or perhaps a gift?'

'No, he did not. Now let me finish,' snapped Colonel Hardy. She continued to read, now through gritted teeth. '*When I received Mr Harris's email yesterday . . .*'

Grace whipped her head round. 'Email?' she mouthed at the cyclops.

Mr Harris avoided eye contact. Instead, he stared intently at Colonel Hardy.

'*. . . and his detailed explanation of how he closed both cases assigned to him so quickly, I said to Norman that I thought we had probably found one of the best assets we've ever had . . .*'

'What?' mouthed Grace, trying to get Mr Harris's attention without Colonel Hardy seeing her.

Colonel Hardy went on, looking pained. '*The fact he tracked our missing judge to Hawaii, when everyone else was convinced of foul play, is staggering!*'

'Yes,' agreed the cyclops. 'Staggering.'

Colonel Hardy fixed her eyes on him. '*And then, to almost single-handedly bring down Bitey Joe when he had taken Grace hostage, was remarkable.*'

'Remarkable,' repeated Mr Harris, nodding.

'*In his email, he even had the good grace to remind me that it wasn't just him, and that he had been assisted by the Hunter family,*' read Colonel Hardy, shaking her head.

'They tried their best,' Mr Harris said quietly.

Colonel Hardy took a deep breath. '*Given Mr Harris's extraordinary efforts, I would like to give him something as a token of my appreciation. First, I would like to promote him, with immediate effect, to the position of . . . WHAT?*' cried Colonel Hardy.

Mr Harris leaned forward, his eye wide and

sparkly with excitement. 'Go on, Patient Lady.'

Colonel Hardy hung her head. '*Senior field officer.*'

'Oh, I thought you were going to say King of England,' said the cyclops, disappointed.

'Senior field officer,' Eamon mouthed from the other side of the table, then mumbled, 'Took me four years of fifteen-hour days to get to senior field officer.'

Colonel Hardy, still holding the Prime Minister's note, looked thoroughly peeved. She walked over to the table and reached for the brown envelope and silver pen. Using the pen to open the envelope, she drew out a shiny catalogue. 'Here,' she snapped, thrusting the catalogue towards him. 'Your token of appreciation from the Prime Minister.'

'A bicycle?' he said, taking the brochure, which
had a shiny, sleek bicycle on the cover. 'A plain
old bicycle?'

'*You* read this and tell him,'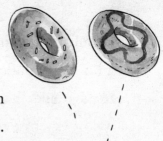
cried Colonel Hardy, wafting
the note that had come from
the envelope under Max's nose.

Max read the note to himself then
cleared his throat. 'You get to choose lots of
bicycles, Mr Harris. When we saw the Prime
Minister last time, after Neville exploded, she
promised she would listen to the issues you
wanted to discuss with her. One of which was
bicycles. Do you remember, you asked her if the
bikes for hire in the city had been chosen by a
troll because of their poor quality?'

Mr Harris tutted. 'Too right. Trolls are cheap,
and those bikes had "troll" written all over them.'

'Well, she has sent this catalogue so you can
choose the bicycles she will replace all the old ones
with,' said Max. 'She wants you to lead the project.
She would like to know if you would be happy
to help.'

What sounded like a muffled sob came from the

general direction of Colonel Hardy.

Mr Harris puffed his chest out self-importantly. 'Yes, I would. It's about time someone with my level of expertise sorted things out. Now, because I didn't get a proper present, can I take this nice silver pen?'

CHAPTER TWENTY-SIX

Party!

When they arrived back at Cake Hunters, Grace let Mr Harris push open the door to the bakery. Colonel Hardy's pen was tucked firmly behind his ear.

'SURPRISE!' yelled Louisa, Danni and Marietto, who were standing by an enormous four-tiered cake. Grace, Frank, Max and Eamon cheered as Kenny clapped enthusiastically from Grace's shoulder.

A banner hung from wall to wall. It read *Well done, Mr Harris*! There were balloons tied in big bunches hanging from every corner of the room, and colourful bunting zigzagged across the bakery.

The cyclops stopped, taking everything in. A wide grin spread across his face.

'It's tradition to have a party to celebrate a Secret Service officer's first closed case, but you closed two at the same time . . . sort of,' said Danni.

'Your methods were more than a little questionable,' said Max. 'But a closed case is a closed case.'

Grace looked at Mr Harris and subtly gestured to everyone around him.

'I suppose I had a bit of help . . .' he muttered begrudgingly. Then he frowned. 'But now I've diligently and expeditiously closed my cases, is that it? Does my job stop? Are you throwing me out of my tiny room?'

'Of course not,' said Louisa. 'You're welcome to stay.'

'Bet you didn't think you'd be saying that to the cyclops that ate us . . .' mumbled Eamon.

'And I'll have another case for you on Monday,' added Max.

'We made you a cake, Mr Harris,' said Danni. 'It has all your favourite things.'

Mr Harris's eyes lit up. 'For me?' He advanced towards it, licking his lips.

'There's no baking powder in it,' said Louisa.

'The bottom tier is chocolate,' explained Danni. 'The next one is salted caramel, then lemon drizzle, then classic Victoria sponge. There are macarons and fairy cakes round the bottom and we've popped some doughnuts and shortbread biscuits on the top.'

'Well now, this is something,' said Mr Harris, walking around it, looking at it from every angle. 'It's not as complicated as a Baumkuchen, or as skilful as a croquembouche – both of which I am planning to make this weekend from the recipes I have found in *Complex Patisserie for Master Bakers* – but it's very . . . entertaining.'

Marietto pointed to the silver board the cake was resting on. 'I 'ave piped a message just 'ere forrr you! I am learning de human ways!'

Mr Harris glanced down and read aloud, '*Congratulations, celebrations and jubilations, Mr*

Harris!' He leaned forward and sniffed the salted caramel layer.

As his tongue started to poke out of his mouth, Grace said, 'Don't lick it! It's for everyone to share!'

The cyclops folded his arms. 'You are a fun hoover. You see fun and you hoover it up. Why must I share all the tiers of my congratulations, celebrations and jubilations cake?'

'Because it's good manners,' said Grace. 'And because we worked as a team.'

Mr Harris frowned. 'I don't see any of *you* with a congratulations, celebrations and jubilations cake.'

'That's because we're sharing yours!' said Grace, grinning. 'Now cut us all a piece please. I'll have chocolate.'

'Wait!' said Mr Harris. 'If I am going to be cutting cake, I will need the proper attire. Let me go and fetch my hat and apron.'

He hurried off up the stairs.

Mr Harris reappeared very quickly. He seemed to be flustered, nervous and excited all at once.

'We're ready for our cake!' said Grace. 'Oh, where is your apron? And your hat?'

'Change of plan,' announced Mr Harris. 'I will be going on a short trip. Please keep my cake safe until I return. I'll take these bits with me. Bye for now!' He produced a grubby blue bag for life from his pocket, plopped the top two tiers of cake into it and shot out of the door.

Danni looked at Louisa. Max looked at Eamon. Grace and Frank looked at each other and shouted in unison, 'Monster Scanner!'

They raced up the stairs and burst into the study. This time, Mr Harris hadn't bothered to try and hide the fact that he had been snooping on the Monster Scanner. The screen blinked with information and the mouse was

dangling from the desk. He had clearly left the room in a hurry.

'He was checking a profile,' said Frank.

Grace grabbed the mouse and scrolled to the top of the screen. As the name came into view, Kenny jumped out of her pocket and onto the desk. He ran to the screen, pointing to the name and then the location.

Grace took in the information. 'Frank, look – Gertrudetta Harris. All this time, he's been searching for his mum,' she said, scrolling down to the location at the bottom of the screen. 'And it would appear that he's found her.'

CHAPTER TWENTY-SEVEN

Gertrudetta

Name: Gertrudetta Millicent Patricia Juanita Mavis Carole Harris

Type: Cyclops

Age: Approximately 427 years

Height: 177 cm

Weight: 214 lb

Strengths: 8 detected: power, caring nature (for a cyclops), healing skills, memory, numeracy, growing vegetables, karate, sudoku.

Weaknesses: 4 detected: fusses too much, naive, holds a grudge, easily led by others.

Likes: Herbs and flowers, natural remedies, horoscopes, brioche, looking after things, her dad Neville (click here for more information), teaching, rollerskating, fractions, algebra, the seaside, recycling.

Dislikes: Microwave meals, seafood, clowns, disloyalty, anything made out of plastic, Scrabble.

Best form of destruction: Pure baking powder or brioche with lots of baking powder in the recipe.

Notes: Unusual personality for a cyclops, as she is capable of love and kindness. Vegetarian. Holds a BIG grudge if someone upsets her. Black belt in karate.

SCORING:

Friendship: 34

Size: 78

Courage: 63

Kindness: 49

Intelligence: 61

Loyalty: 68

Violence: 39

Danger: 65

Type: RARE (mainly due to unusual personality for a cyclops)

Location: Secret Cave, Forest of Fiends, Monster World

The End

(until next time . . .)

What will Grace and Mr Harris get up to next?

Read on for a sneak peek at the next book

in the series . . .

CHAPTER ONE

Where is Mr Harris?

Grace felt the stepladder wobble slightly as she got to the top. She passed the shiny red cherry to Kenny, her faithful little Key Catcher, who took it in his wiry hands and immediately leapt off her shoulder. He glided through the air smoothly, popping the cherry on to the top of an enormous profiterole mountain as he passed it. He landed neatly on the other side of the table and took a bow.

'Well done, Kenny!' said Grace. 'I would never have had a steady enough hand to get that all the way up there. It's the biggest profiterole mountain I've ever seen.'

'It needs to be,' said Grace's older sister Danni, wiping her hands on her yellow apron. 'It'll be feeding over two hundred people at a wedding. I never want to see a profiterole again!'

'I'm actually glad Mr Harris isn't here,' said Grace. 'He wouldn't be able to resist the profiteroles. We'd be replacing them every three seconds."

'Is he still not answering his video phone?' said Danni, frowning.

Grace shook her head. 'I haven't been able to get hold of him since he left the party yesterday. I'm starting to get a bit worried.'

'He's a massive, rude, people-eaty cyclops,' said Danni. 'I'm sure he's fine. Have you found out any more about where he's heading?'

'W-well, we know he's gone to look for his m-mum, Gertrudetta,' said Frank, peering round from behind the profiterole mountain. 'And we know she lives in some sort of s-secret cave in the F-Forest of Fiends, in Monster World. The journey there is likely to be d-dangerous.'

Grace nodded. 'From what we've found out on the Monster Scanner, there are woods and bridges and ravines, and goodness knows what else, to get past on the way to the forest. And you know how easily distracted he is! He'll be hungry, or tired, or bored, and he'll do something stupid, I know it.'

'Well, at least he took some of his celebration cake with him,' said Danni. 'At least that will mean he's not hungry for a while.'

Grace sighed. 'Yes, probably for about five minutes,' she said, sighing. 'I'm going to try phoning him again. Perhaps if I tell him about the profiteroles, he'll come back.'

Danni shook her head vigorously as Grace pressed the redial button on the video phone and waited.

Just as she was about to hang up, a large yellowish eye filled the screen.

'What do you want, Doughnut Lady?' Mr Harris barked.

'Finally!' said Grace. 'I've been trying to get hold of you for hours! You left at the very start of your party, Mr Harris! If you'd just told us you were going to find your mum, we'd have come with you!'

The cyclops's glare filled the small screen. 'Didn't take you long to snoop on where I was going, did it?' he snapped.

'You didn't hide it very well!" Grace retorted. "Now, come back. Let's do this properly.'

The cyclops snorted. 'Properly? You're a monster hunter, I'm hardly going to lead you to my own flesh and blood!'

Frank squeezed his face in next to Grace's on the video phone and piped up, 'You're a m-monster hunter too.' The ornate golden fork he carried everywhere for protection glinted in the corner of the screen.

Mr Harris shook his head in

disgust. 'No, I'm not, Shrimp Boy. I'm a monster. The BEST monster! And, also, a recently-promoted Secret Service Senior Field Officer. The BEST Secret Service Senior Field Officer! I multi-task,' He grinned self-importantly.

'Exactly!' said Grace. 'So, what if you're needed here? You might be given another case today!'

'You can do it, I'm very busy,' said Mr Harris dismissively. Then his eye opened wider. 'What's that behind you? Is it a mountain of profiteroles?'

Grace swung round so the chocolatey choux buns were out of sight. 'Oh, that's nothing, it's fake, you know, just for display. So, what exactly are you doing at the moment?' she asked, trying to get a glimpse behind the massive cyclops. 'And *where* are you?'

'I'm staying with an associate before I embark on my journey,' he replied. 'And now I must go. So, stop phoning me, and annoying me, and . . .'

'Mr 'Arris! Come 'ere! I 'ave

another amazing flavourrr for you to trrry!' came an Italian-accented voice from somewhere behind Mr Harris.

'You're with Marietto! You're eating ice cream!' cried Grace.

'Shhhh,' hissed the cyclops. 'Don't you dare ruin this for me. I've tried forty-four flavours of ice cream and I am NOT stopping now. He cannot know you're trying to track me down. He'll hand me over in a second! I've never known a Gelato Guzzler that's so well-behaved and sensible. He's ridiculous and the most un-monstery monster in history. But, he makes excellent ice cream so go away, Doughnut Lady. I'm about to try double chocolate coconut swirl with just a hint of Earl Grey. I've been waiting for ages to get to this one. And you, with your beaky nose and your snoopy little eyes and your meddling computer fingers, are not going to stop me.'

He hung up.

'He seems perfectly fine,' said Danni.

Frank nodded. 'Very n-normal.'

'He's a pain in the neck,' said Grace. 'But if he's eating ice cream, he's going nowhere for a while. And that means we have a bit more time to research the Forest of Fiends, before we actually have to go down that rickety ladder to Monster World and find him ourselves.'

MONSTER GLOSSARY

Baby Prodder

You know when a baby goes the same colour as a beetroot and screams for absolutely NO reason, and passers-by tut and huff and point at their parents? That crimson baby will almost certainly have been poked by a Baby Prodder. Why? Well, mainly because Baby Prodders are mean. And also because they have terrible hearing so no screeching baby will ever bother them one little bit. They have long index fingers and reddish eyes. They like wearing old-fashioned baby bonnets when out on a baby-prodding extravaganza.

Bath Dweller

Related to Slime Imps, Bath Dwellers are a similar texture but have a multitude of tentacles. Invisible to most adults, they are often the reason small children scream their heads off at the mere mention of a nice soak in the bath.

Bottom Biter

A fearsome cross between a Shadow Stalker and a Mutant Vampire Bat, Bottom Biters are one of the rarest members of the vampire family. They are quick, strong, confident, generally unkind and very, very bitey. And because they love to bite things, most have a strange fascination for food. While most of them love a good BBQ, some have been known to develop a liking for more unusual food groups, such as cheese, shellfish, pulses and puddings.

Button Gobbler

Lost another button? Button Gobblers will pick them directly off your coat or your school shirt with their razor-sharp teeth. Don't bother looking for the ones that disappear either, they will have been digested within seconds.

Coin Clincher

These funny little creatures are a bit like Monster World magpies because they love shiny things, especially coins. They will shoot directly towards anything that looks like a dropped coin and immediately drop it into the pouch they have on the front of their tummies (a little like the one in which a kangaroo carries its baby). Unsurprisingly, they enjoy spending time in shopping centres, arcades and banks. Some are even known to live inside the 2p pusher machines that can be found in seaside arcades – so next time you triumphantly scoop up your winnings, just check there isn't a grumpy looking Coin Clincher nestling in amongst them.

Cyclops

One-eyed and usually very large, cyclopes made regular appearances in Greek and Roman mythology. Since then, they've evolved in a fascinating way. While most are still as thick as custard, some have gained in intelligence. Most are self-important, some are power-crazed and many are happy to eat the problems they are presented with, especially if those problems are gate-keeping trolls. Cyclopes love board games, bicycles and sweet treats.

Drain Dribbler

It used to be thought that these grotty, spitty monsters didn't serve much of a purpose until a research paper, written by Mr E. Hunter in February 1999, changed that thinking. Generally found drooling into drains in Monster World, the dribble belonging to these sluggish, blobby

monsters actually contains chemicals that break down the waste found deep inside drains (urgh). So while much of Monster World is dank, dusty and disorganised, its plumbing and drainage systems are absolutely splendid.

Fossil Finder

Found almost solely in locations steeped in history and museums, these small, winged creatures are obsessed with the notion of finding ancient things and keeping them. Many have extensive collections that the Natural History Museum would snap their claws off for. Others have stolen their collections *from* the Natural History Museum – but the less said about that the better.

Gelato Guzzler

These monsters are quite rare. They are generally only found in Italy or in specific parts of Monster World itself. They are flamboyant and kind, ready to make friends with almost anyone and anything. Show too much interest and you will hear their life story (their lifespan is several hundred years, so don't say you weren't warned) while being force-fed the most delicious ice

Gelato Guzzler - - - -

cream you've ever tasted. Their four arms make them excellent multi-taskers. Rumour has it that some live and work quite freely in many Italian cities, which explains the AMAZING gelato.

Most Italian humans don't question the four arms, they just appreciate the ice cream they get to take to their nonna's every Sunday.

Grease Gobbler

These are slimy, blubbery monsters who are mostly found living in fish and chip shops, burger vans and fast-food restaurants. They are at their happiest when cleaning their habitats with their mop-like tongues.

Hair Knotter

Anyone who has long hair will understand the agony of brushing it first thing in the morning. How does it get so knotty? You've been asleep, lying still, for goodness' sake! The answer is Hair Knotters. While you're asleep these tangly teasers hop onto your head and quite literally tie your hair into knots. They are often found in pairs, with their sidekick, a Hairband Thief and guess what these monsters do when your hair is finally knot-free and you've stopped begging your mum to leave you alone? They flick your hair bands as far away as possible.

Hair Knotter - -

YEE HAW!

Handbag Hider

Guess where Handbag Hiders like to conceal themselves? That's right, in the fridge! Ha! Of course they don't! They hide in handbags, as their name suggests. Small and able to change colour like a chameleon, they can blend into any handbag, of any colour and size. Once inside, they cause havoc. They'll take the lids off lip balm so it gets covered in fluff and hair, unzip coin purses so every last penny falls to the very bottom of the bag, blow their noses in any nice clean tissues they find and eat all the lurking sweets and chewing gum.

- - - Handbag Hider

Impatience Booster

These monsters tend to come in swarms and will gravitate quite naturally to where there are queues of people. They carry little aerosols in their pudgy paws which are full of their natural odour (like our sweat, yuck). This substance is undetectable to human noses but causes even the most patient and fun individuals to be irritable and bored within seconds. So next time you're queuing for popcorn at the cinema and your dad snaps your head off because you want salty *and* sweet, have a look for a small, chubby hand, carrying an aerosol, poking out from behind the chocolate buttons.

Key Catcher

By far the most helpful and loyal species of monster, Key Catchers are affectionate, brave, resilient and strong, despite their tiny size and wire-like build. They make excellent companions and are especially useful if you are the sort of person who forgets your keys and regularly locks themselves out of the house. Key Catchers can lock and unlock anything in seconds. They also have a mischievous streak and will sometime play tricks on humans, hanging on to a key from inside a lock. So, when your Uncle Brian is sprinting towards the cupboard that holds his fifteen-year old can of WD40, just hold a cornflake cake by

the sticky lock. Key Catchers love them, it'll be out in seconds, leaving Uncle Brian completely baffled at how you unlocked the door he quietly cursed at.

Mutant Vampire Bat

The clue is in the title. These are vampire bats where something has gone badly wrong. Sometimes it's their hairstyle, sometimes it's the size of their wings. Other times it's the fact that they will sink their mutant fangs into your neck quicker than you can say, 'Do you know Dracula?'

Pant Parader

These monsters are fascinated by a good sturdy pair of human pants, favouring those worn by old people. They consider them an excellent accessory for every occasion. If worn on their head, their brightly coloured hair is generally pulled through the leg holes. If worn correctly, they will always be pulled on over the top of any other clothing the Pant Parader has selected, which will be seen as an inferior garment. Even if it's threaded with gold.

Pant Parader - - - -

Parent Punisher

These are interesting and rebellious monsters. They don't take kindly to children being told off so when this sort of unpleasant scenario occurs, they will almost always do something to take revenge against the teller-offer. Whether it's a tiny poo in the coffee granules, or a quick wipe of a toothbrush round the toilet, these creatures are known for their loyalty to kids everywhere, and their wild creativity in punishments.

- - - Parent Punisher

Pickpocket Pixie

If you don't know what an aye-aye monkey's fingers look like, Google it NOW! Got a picture? Those freakishly long-fingered hands are an exact replica of a Pickpocket Pixie's, just slightly bigger. They flutter round soundlessly, poking their hands into pockets, shopping bags, rucksacks and purses. They will pilfer anything. They just like other people's things, whether it's a diamond ring, an old shopping list, a snotty tissue or a half-eaten Mars bar.

Pie Pincher

Pie Pinchers lurk around bakeries and the pastry section in supermarkets. There is no pie that this funny little beast won't pinch. Apple, cherry, pecan, chicken and ham, steak and ale, butternut squash and asparagus – anything with a pastry lid is at risk.

Poo Shuffler

Have you ever trodden in a dog poo you just didn't see? You probably only found out because you trod it into the carpet when you got home and your parents went nuts. Poo Shufflers do exactly what their name suggests. They shuffle poos into your path, watch the consequences and laugh. A lot.

Roof Ruiners

Hurricanes are not the largest cause of roof tiles flying off houses. Fact. Roof Ruiners often swirl around in huge groups creating havoc. In formation, they are often mistaken for tornados. When on their own, they tend to throw caution to the wind (excuse the pun) and often sit on top of their roof of choice, brazenly picking off tiles and seeing how far they can throw them. They enjoy warm temperatures and often gravitate to South America as a result of this.

Shadow Stalker

Ever had that funny feeling something's watching you pick your nose, or lurking in the shadows of your brother's stinky bedroom, or chasing you up the stairs – even though there's nothing there? Well, mostly, there isn't, so get a grip! But sometimes, in extreme cases, it's a Shadow Stalker. Don't worry, they can't hurt anyone and they can only exist where there are shadows, but they can make their presence felt, and that's enough for most of us to be turning every light on in the house immediately FOREVER.

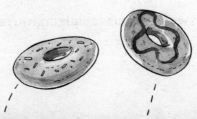

Snack Snaffler

These large-handed creatures will eat anything. Crisps, biscuits, sweets, they're not fussy (although they're not keen on rice cakes – too bland). If you're snacking on it, they will try and steal it. Or they'll lurk under your seat in the hope you'll drop something.

Snack Snaffler - - -

Snot-nosed Ogre

Snot-nosed Ogres are large and not very clever. As their name would suggest, they have constantly runny noses, which makes them very angry creatures. They are known to enjoy a good punch-up and they like eating the odd human or large mammal. Luckily, they can be distracted by shiny objects, kaleidoscopes or ice cream. If you happen to have all three of those things with you, you'll probably make a snotty friend for life.

Trinket Trader

Arch-enemies of Fossil Finders, Trinket Traders enjoy finding valuable things and selling them on to auction houses and second-hand shops. They frequent antique markets and museums, and are distinguishable by their huge eyes which often sit behind even huger glasses (whether they need them or not).

Trinket Trader - - -

Tripper Upper

You know when you trip over absolutely nothing, and your mum says you're clumsy? Well, it's probably not you being clumsy, it's more than likely a Tripper Upper being mischievous. These monsters camouflage into whichever floor they are lurking on and think it's hilarious when they pop up and trip you over.

Troll (Freak-footed)

These are unusual... Thank goodness! Freak-footed trolls feet can grow up to twice the length of their entire bodies. Their toes are often long and webbed with deadly claws protruding from the ends. Unlike their gate-keeping cousins, they have no interest in sticking to the rules and will happily use violence to resolve issues. They mostly like to use their claws or stamp on those who annoy them, although they have also been known to use the unbearable, blue cheese-like stench that emanates from their freakish hooves to simply render their enemies unconscious.

Troll (Gate-keeping)

Now, if you know anything about trolls, you'll know many of them take jobs in the security industry. Why? Because they like to feel important, boss people around, make up rules and sometimes, if the mood takes them, wear bomber jackets with walkie talkies clipped to them. They are generally excellent at their jobs because they refuse to believe they could ever be wrong and, trust me, if your name isn't on the list, you're not going in. (Unless you're Mr Harris, and then you eat them to overcome their efficiency and quickly resolve the issue.)

Troll (Human posing as)

There has only been one of these recorded since 1927 and you may have just read about him in this book. How he survived even a few days in Monster World is extraordinary, as he did everything wrong. He was pleasant, he smiled with his very white teeth, he relaxed the rules and said 'please' and 'thank you'. If he'd been there even an hour longer, it's highly likely a number of monsters would have become highly suspicious... and who knows what would have happened then.

Troll - - -

Vegetable Nibbler

If you know someone who grows vegetables in their garden, you may well have heard them shout, 'What is eating my cabbages?! Why are there tooth marks in my cauliflower?!'. They will blame rabbits, slugs, snails, birds and sometimes even their neighbours. They're wrong. Vegetable Nibblers are almost always responsible.

MONSTER PROFILE

Name: Gianna Pollero

Type: Author

Age: 43 years

Height: 5'2"

Weight: Not telling you.

Strengths: 4 detectable: kindness, sense of adventure, writing skills (hopefully) and sense of humour.

Weaknesses: 3 detectable: jelly sweets, cute animals, home décor shops.

Likes: Reading, writing, chocolate, animals, gardening, photography, arty things, coffee, Italy, interior design, architecture and fruit jellies.

Dislikes: Rudeness, artichokes, anyone unkind, being cold and wasps.

Best form of destruction: One tonne of jelly sweets. I will eat them and explode.

NOTES: This monster likes to curl up with a cup of coffee and a book on a regular basis. When disturbed, she's very grumpy.

SCORING:

Friendship: 100

Size: 40

Courage: 62

Kindness: 93

Intelligence: 76

Loyalty: 90

Violence: 0

Danger: 5

Type: MEDIUM RARE

MONSTER PROFILE

Name: Sarah Horne

Type: Illustrator

Age: Unknown. Experts guess between 0–862 years old.

Height: 5'6"

Weight: Somewhere between a flea and a sumo wrestler.

Strengths: Can draw pretty much anything, joy, compassion, fun.

Weaknesses: Stationery, Tuc biscuits or any manner of biscuit.

Likes: Drawing silly things, running up hills, Fruit and Nut chocolate, music and a good poo joke.

Dislikes: Lies, impatient drivers and seaweed.

Best form of destruction: Too much chit-chatting about nothing at all.

Notes: A Sarah is an elusive creature. In the wild she can be found painting large canvases. A Sarah is especially drawn to joy and whimsy, stories (especially the silly ones) and she loves creative, big-picture people.

SCORING:

Friendship: 100

Size: 55

Courage: 71

Kindness: 90

Intelligence: 72

Loyalty: 95

Violence: 0

Danger: 0.000000001

Acknowledgements

A huge thank you, first and foremost, to Oscar and Sophia, who read this book chapter by chapter as I wrote it. They laughed in all the right places, made some invaluable suggestions and solved more than one plot-hole between them. They are nothing short of amazing and I am so incredibly lucky to have them by my side throughout these wonderful book-writing journeys.

Thanks to my lovely mum, Lesley, who is unbelievably supportive and brilliant, as well as being the best mum I could possibly ask for.

Very special thanks to my bestie, Maria, who, amongst many other things, provided the excellent name 'Bitey Joe' for the villainous Bottom Biter in this story. And to Amelie, for the awesome Pant Parader monster!

I am beyond grateful to my fabulous friends

who unfailingly support me, encourage me and hold my hand when I need them to – Helen, Tracey, Lindsay, Gemma, Annmarie, Jo, Aarti, Carly (and the Johnson clan), Gillian, Clare, Rachel, Hannah, Claire, Paul, Richard, Ruth, Lynne, Julie and so many others (including all the others at Valley Invicta Academies Trust who have gone above and beyond to help me). Thank you. So much.

I am truly blessed to have the best agent and editor I could possibly ask for. Rachel – enormous, overflowing bucket-fulls of thanks to you and to all at the Jo Unwin Literary Agency. You are all just gorgeous and I wouldn't be loving every minute of doing what I'm doing without you. Georgia – thank you so much for making everything so easy, for being a complete delight to work with and for spotting all the things I really should just have done in the first place! I know, without a doubt, that you 'get' my characters and my stories, and that means the world. Thank you too, to Piccadilly

Press for providing the loveliest of literary homes for my books. I am beyond happy to be a part of the Bonnier family.

I would also like to take this opportunity to thank new friends, gained through the warm world of the writing community – there are many of you but, Eddy and Anton in particular, you've been so helpful in getting my books out there. I'm truly grateful.

And now the really important bit – a massive, Mr Harris-size thank you to all my wonderful readers. I will never tire of hearing what you thought of the stories, listening to you talk about the characters as though you know them yourselves, and seeing the delight on your faces when Poo Shufflers are mentioned.

A few years ago, the thought of going into a bookshop and seeing my own book was something I could only dream about and hope for.

Now, I am so, so lucky that it's a reality, and I genuinely couldn't be happier or more grateful.